The Familialists

TJ Madden

SLASHIC HORROR PRESS

Other Titles by TT Madden

The Cosmic Color Student Bodies

Gorman's House

places where you cannot be: an afro-american travel guide

The Neon Revelation

The Shapes of Our Screams

Forthcoming

No Chains Will Ever Hold Us: Tales of Identity Horror

Dream of the Machine Child (working title)

Praise for The Familialists

"Days after reading, I still found myself thinking back on *The Familialists* in the quiet moments of my day. Not only is the horror fresh and inventive, the story is impactful... Painfully beautiful. Madden's writing will get under your skin, through your skull, and ignite something new."
– Will Rogers, co-host of the Guide to the Unknown podcast

"Just when you thought it was safe to yearn for the good old days, here comes TT Madden with a dark kaleidoscope of domestic horror. Stifling, claustrophobic, and oppressive as all hell, *The Familialists* exposes nostalgia as a many-mouthed monster... Each chapter's got teeth that won't let go."
– Jacob Steven Mohr, author of The Unwelcome

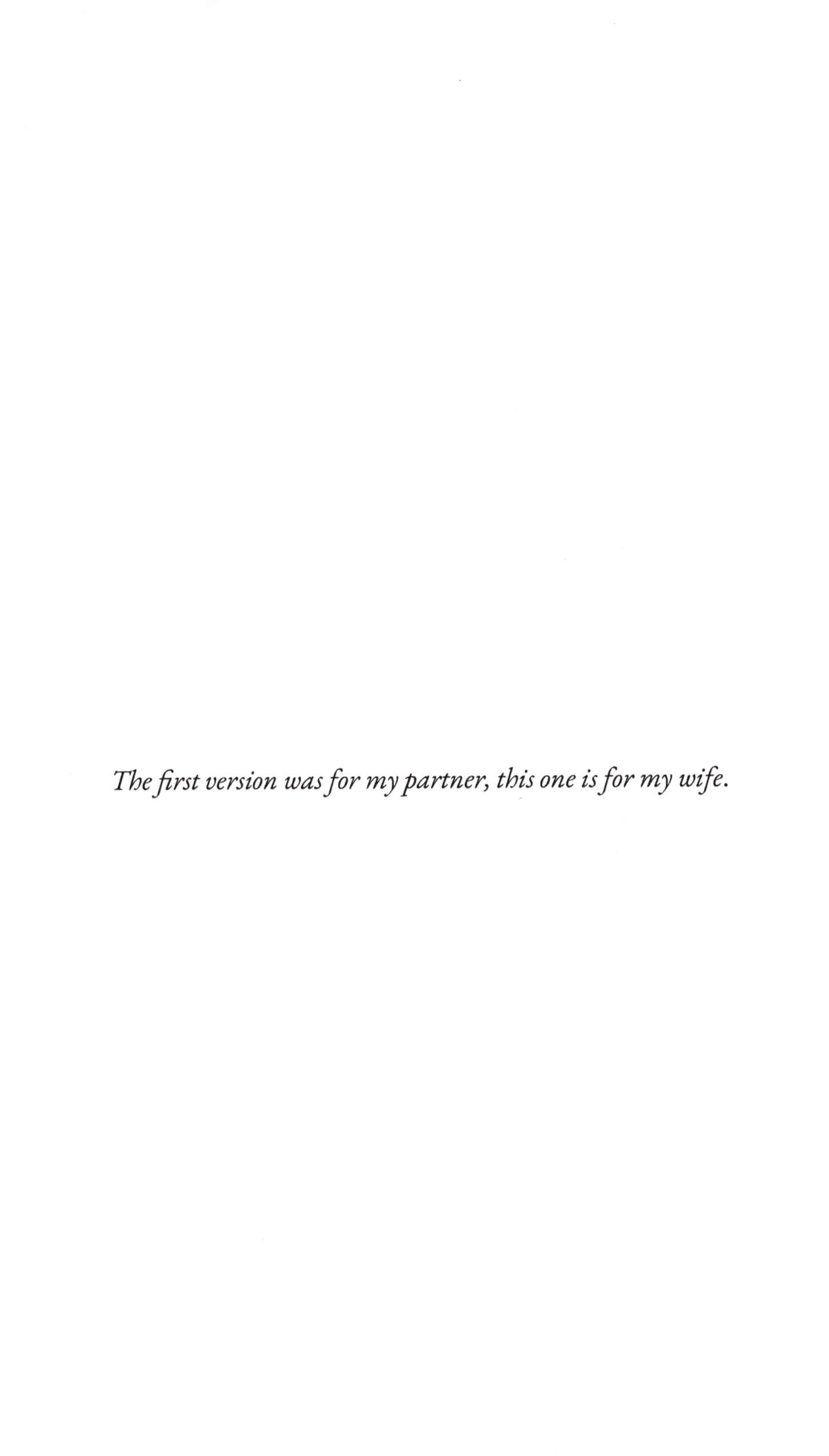

The first version was for my partner, this one is for my wife.

Some things are so horrific that truth isn't sufficient for the truth. The only way to convey it is with fiction so outlandish that it approximates the absurdity of true horror.

Tim O'Brien

part I

Amuse-Bouche

JUNE 19, 2024

Sorrel thinks it must be a dream when she sees Maud again. Sorrel's crossing the parking lot towards Beekman's Diner, in the middle of putting her curls up rather than having them hang down around her face. It's not a way to stay invisible, but the hair is a clearer signifier of her heritage. Her skin is one thing, but people look past that all the time; mixed, she's brown enough to be considered tan, brown enough to blend in. The frizz in her hair after being in a kitchen, though, that's like a bright neon sign signifying who she really is, and by extension, how the world has been taught to treat her.

Sorrel is thinking about this, only paying attention to the woman in her peripheral when it seems like she might bump into her halfway up the diner steps. As they pass one another in the entrance, she looks up, dodges to avoid her, and sees Maud.

The woman Sorrel used to know is dressed like a 1950s housewife; a red sun-dress with white polka-dots, matching red heels, and a similar shock of bloody red across her lips. Her blond hair is done up in a tight bun, and she's even wearing one of those sweaters around her shoulders, buttoned at the neck, her arms not actually through the sleeves. Her porcelain skin glows in the dappled sunlight and time itself seems to stop around Sorrel just as it did the very first time she ever laid eyes on her.

Is it really you? Points of sweat pierce Sorrel's brown skin, the very same way they did when she first looked at Maud years ago, when she first walked into the classroom; under her arms, at the small of her back, and between her breasts. She hated that last one, especially.

It must be a dream, Sorrel thinks, must be someone else. She hasn't seen Maud in years. Not since that night, the one she's tried to forget. The life she's tried to get past. A kaleidoscope of feeling smashes through her as she watches Maud walk past. As she starts to understand that she's in her proximity again.

So close.

Close enough to touch, and that makes Sorrel remember the sight of her brown skin against Maud's porcelain, the contrast she enjoyed so much for some reason she could never articulate. She's sweating even more now, realizes she's leaning against the steps' railing so she doesn't swoon.

"Maud?" The name whispers out from her lips before she can stop it. Sorrel has no plan when she says her name. She is driven purely by instinct, by id, by body and memory, and all she knows is she has to be here in front of her. Her legs are weak, like the first time she ever laid eyes on her, and all the other times since.

Maud hesitates, stops at the bottom of the diner steps, standing there with her bags of takeout. She blinks. "I'm sorry?"

Sorrel's mouth is dry. Why didn't she think of anything before she just blurted something out like an idiot? But then she wonders how she *could* have thought of anything. She never could think straight in front of Maud. She wishes it could have been more like the first time.

I'm Sorrel.

Yes. I know who you are.

For a moment Sorrel thinks maybe she's made a mistake, that this is a different woman. A natural doppelgänger. Someone who just looks incredibly like Maud, but isn't. The way she's dressed, it seems possible. Her clothes are so far afield of how Maud used to dress. But it's been a long time. People change.

Especially after what they've been through.

A change might've been just what Maud needed to put the past behind her. But Sorrel knows she'd recognize those hot-red lips anywhere. Maud always wore that color. No matter the rest of her outfit. Those red lips always drew Sorrel's eye. She remembers hoping she'd be able to catch a glimpse of Maud's tongue between them as she opened them for a drink of water, or to pull a bit of food off her fork. She remembers those red lips she remembers coming closer and closer to her face, that bubbling feeling she realized so late wasn't in her stomach.

But the clincher, the thing that proves to her it's Maud, beyond the shadow of a doubt, is her eyes. Maud, down in the parking lot, looks up at Sorrel, on the steps of the diner, the way you'd look up at a stranger, nothing more, and Sorrel sees it in her eyes.

It's her. Maud.

It's *her* Maud.

There's a glitch in the universe for a moment, the briefest of illusions where it seems like this dreamscape is going to stop, break apart, and return everything to the reality that should be. The moment where it seems to Sorrel like Maud is going to recognize her. Where there's going to be a change in the way things are going, a reversion to the way they were. But after that shudder the world's walls hold up and Maud smiles at Sorrel in that kind-but-ultimately-meaningless way reserved for strangers on the street.

She turns, aborting the conversation, and crosses the parking lot towards a shiny, retro convertible with its top down. It's loud and bright, as equally '50s as Maud is dressed, like how people in the past imagined cars were going to look in the future; big, curving wheel wells and bright, primary colors.

Before Sorrel knows it, before she can regret it, she's standing in front of the woman who cannot be—who *has* to be. She says her name; "Sorrel. You remember me." She wants to say it like a statement, hoping it'll be the nudge Maud needs, but it comes out like a question. Sorrel has a deep voice, like a lifelong smoker's even though she's only ever hit a couple joints in high school. She remembers all the times Maud made her whisper when they talked, all the times she said she wanted to hear Sorrel's throat purr close to her ear.

Please, Sorrel begs, she doesn't know who, *don't have forgotten me. Please, God, don't have forgotten about us.*

Sorrel can see the gears inside Maud's head winding and clanking, trying to recall her. Why is this so hard to remember, she wonders. Was she, was their time together, of so little consequence to Maud when it meant everything in the world to Sorrel?

Then, an idea.

"Sti em lerros." It sounds like gibberish, but a very deliberate gibberish. It's something even Sorrel hasn't thought about in years; their idioglossia. Their child-language. A backwards-speech they made up as girls. What she means is *It's me, Sorrel.*

She sees the instant recognition on Maud's face. The veneer cracks, and Sorrel sees her in there, past all the 1950s doll makeup. The Maud she remembers. The Maud she still loves, after all the years and all the trials. The one who didn't get away, but who was taken. Yes, of course it's her. Maud remembers. She even wobbles in place as if the realization has physically struck her. Sorrel reaches out a hand to help her, but Maud holds her own up to refuse. Takes half a step back.

That's when Sorrel sees it; the wedding ring. It's a *rock*, a huge diamond glinting against the sun. Sorrel barely has time to process it before there's a man at Maud's side, a man steadying her, a man's hands where Sorrel has had hers, where she wants them again; on Maud's elbow and the small of her back, holding her up. He, too, looks a little dated. A little retro. He's wearing a gray suit, but not a modern one. A little shaggier-looking, the fit bigger than today's style. Like he just stepped out of a noir movie into the modern world. There's a bright orange flower on his lapel.

He asks Maud, "Are you alright, darling?"

The man looks like Cary Grant; tall, a little lanky, broad-shouldered, hair slicked to one side. Sorrel feels...woozy when she looks at him. Like she's just taken a shot of something strong. If she's being honest, there's a part of her that's inexplicably attracted to him, that wants him to take her up, take her *like a man*, wrap his arms around her waist and pull her close and plant a big, strong kiss on her lips while she leans back, one foot plucked up off the ground. The thought feels invasive, like it's not just not hers, but one he put into her.

Who are you? she wonders both of the man and herself. She takes a step back, hoping whatever this effect is, it might be based on proximity, and she can escape it.

"Yes," Maud says to him. "Yes, John, I'm fine. I just got a little faint there for a moment."

"Let me help you." The man—John—helps Maud to the convertible, and Sorrel follows like a lovestruck puppy dog. Maud puts the food in the back and John opens her door for her, like a gentleman, making sure she's buckled in before he turns back to Sorrel and acknowledges her for the first time.

"Thank you, sweetheart, but we're quite alright." He says as much, but when he does, Sorrel doesn't think anything is alright. Something settles in the pit of her stomach. Something heavy and awful. John smiles at her, but it's like a chimpanzee's smile; not a greeting, a warning. The kind of smile that doesn't reach his eyes. Eyes that a moment ago Sorrel found deep and dreamy, but now she sees as reptilian, unblinking.

John hustles to the front of the convertible, leaving Sorrel to become vacuumed into that empty space where he once stood, so she can be closer to Maud. She seems woozy too, out of place. She takes a moment to catch her breath before looking up at Sorrel and smiling briefly. She reaches a hand out and touches Sorrel's arm.

"Thank you for your assistance, hun," she says as John starts up the engine, her hand sliding down Sorrel's arm towards her fingers. Maud flashes Sorrel a smile like John's, one that was very human, but equally as wrong, as she places something in Sorrel's hand. Discreetly. "*Pleh em.*" And then the convertible is pulling out of the parking lot, out into traffic, and it's gone, leaving Sorrel standing there alone, looking down at what she realizes is a handful of pomegranate seeds, faced with the horror what she's just heard.

Maud, speaking back to her in that language Sorrel knew she remembered.

Help me.

WHAT YOU WANT TO BE, OR WHAT YOU WANT

Sorrel has to start her shift at Beekman's Diner, but her mind is elsewhere. It's obvious from her performance. Simple things slip her mind. She listens, but she doesn't really hear. She has to ask for orders more than once, tries to blame the cacophony of the breakfast rush. Basic motor functions are kaput. People who are ordinarily dismissive of her because she's of mixed race, or because she's a woman, or because she's in the food service industry, are now dismissive of her for performance-based reasons.

Pleh em.

All she can think of is Maud, and the pomegranate seeds in her pocket. Of all the things to slip her, all the things to make sure she got, why fucking pomegranate seeds? All-day breakfast and fussy toddlers and unnecessarily-hyper-specific coffee orders carry no importance with the weight of what she's witnessed, of who she never thought she'd see again, and the confusion of those last couple moments.

Where have you been?

Sorrel remembers what it was like the last time she ever saw Maud. The image of her and her running mascara, her puffy eyes, crouching on the roof just outside Sorrel's childhood bedroom window, has been forever burned into her consciousness. A time in her life she swore she'd never forget. A time she struggles to always remember. Maud was being moved away. Her parents found out about their affair. That was what they'd called it too: an affair. Like they were each married women and not high schoolers in their first real, first true relationship.

Beekman's is just a few blocks away from the neighborhood of Gough's Cove, where the hot rod disappeared into, and Sorrel spends half her shift looking longingly in that direction. Out windows. Standing on the edge of the parking lot when she brings a car their call-ahead order. Eyes drifting over when she's carrying armfuls of plates, supposed to be watching where she's going.

There must be a way back. Sorrel remembers thinking the same thing in those initial empty weeks without Maud. Those few weeks after the end of a first teenage love where it feels like the world will end. There had to be something that could bring the two of them back together. But weeks turned into months. And then the months turned into years. And Maud became, instead of a living, breathing woman, the memory of a person. Someone Sorrel once knew. And then maybe even a figment of her imagination, a fantasy.

Is that why Sorrel has such a longing for her now? The rose-colored glasses of memory? The even more powerful ones of imagination? Their relationship was not perfect, but it feels like it was. Like there was nothing in the world except for them. Isn't that how all first loves feel?

Or do first out-of-the-closet loves feel different, more special?

Sorrel doesn't smoke, but she's heard it calms nerves or something. With Maud's coded plea for help ringing through her ears, Sorrel really, really needs to calm down. She bums a cigarette off the line cook in the afternoon, out behind the diner. It does nothing to calm her nerves and she realizes it's all another lie, like so many other parts of the world. She leans against the side of the building, pulls her sagging curls back up into a bun in a semi-successful attempt to rid the back of her neck of sweat, dragging on the cigarette and trying to inhale. But her leg still bounces. Her eyes still dart all around. Her fingertips still flutter.

Pleh em.

"Why do people even smoke these?" she grumbles more to herself as she stubs out the half-smoked butt on the side of the building, feeling anger rise in her chest. She heads back inside for another cup of coffee, already feeling the little ball of thorns that convinces her to make bad decisions knotting itself around in her guts. If calming techniques weren't going to work, maybe she could overcorrect, get herself to caffeine-crash, and that would get some of this off of her. There's a part of Sorrel that knows better.

Therapy language would tell her this is self-sabotage, but that ball of thorns writhes and screams and demands to be fed.

It's the same impulse that got her involved with Maud in the first place.

Maud had joined her school in the middle of Sorrel's junior year, and whenever Sorrel looked across the classroom at her, it wasn't like when someone looked at their soon-to-be-love in the movies; a single moment where time slowed and music played. It wasn't triumphant, transcendent. No particles of light swirled around Maud when Sorrel looked at her. What she felt instead was something almost sinister. A forbidden feeling. A deep and sensational jealousy in the pit of her stomach. Something that caused her to squirm when they passed one another in the hall, to cross her ankles under her chair whenever Maud walked into the classroom, to hang her head low as if other people could see the envy written across her face.

Sorrel would look away at every opportunity, every time she found herself staring, lost in her fascination with Maud's body. Look away. But just as quickly she would always look back. She saw her across the cafeteria, talking with another group of students, the center of everyone's attention. Sorrel found herself thinking of the way Maud's long, straight hair flowed, and wondered what it would feel like having hair like that, the sensation of it touching the small of her back, instead of the curls so many adults to her were unprofessional. She saw Maud on the field hockey oval and found herself staring at her exposed legs, muscles bunching as she ran. She thought about what it would be like to be that fit, instead of the layer of baby fat she still had. She thought about having skin that wasn't always compared to food while she dragged her feet to her next class, hidden in oversized sweats like she always was, hiding the body that so many people felt the need to comment on.

She saw her in the shower after gym class.

And then Sorrel finally understood what she was feeling was only a half-truth, that she wanted to be like her. But even more... She wanted her.

Standing up in the middle of the staff bathroom, having retreated to the only place she has privacy, she stuffs the pomegranate seeds into her mouth, aware of the absurdity of her position. Hoping to feel something. She doesn't.

HOME AGAIN, HOME AGAIN

MAUD TRIES AN EXERCISE she knows but can't remember ever learning. She distills her emotions down to their basest forms possible. Turns them into short, simple questions. What are you feeling? Who or what made you feel this way? Why? Maud has the answers to only the first couple of questions.

What is she feeling? Upset.

Who or what made her feel that way? The brown girl at the diner (*Sorrel*).

Why is she feeling that way? No idea.

Maud has no idea why, either, that an intrusive little voice keeps surfacing in the back of her head, a voice that reminds her that she keeps thinking of the *woman* from the diner as a *girl*. Maud never referred to adult men as boys. Is it some mannerism she picked up from John?

Did he behave that way towards the woman because she was a woman or because she was brown? That little voice cuts through her thoughts, and Maud wonders why she would ever think something so cruel about her husband. *Because it's warranted.*

Maud is so lost in this sudden onrush of intrusive thoughts that she doesn't register the moment they arrive back in Trinity Springs. They're just there. Back home on Bender Circle. Lawn perfectly-manicured, flowers arranged beautifully in their beds, their gardeners' effects seen, but themselves invisible, just like they should be.

Why would you think that?

Maud can hear children playing somewhere in the distance, but she can't see them. An American flag hangs tall from a pole in their front garden and she can smell someone grilling somewhere in the neighborhood. The temperature is just cool enough to justify the sweater around her shoulders, and the breeze just calm enough to keep her hair in place. It's all perfect. Perfect. Is it, though? Why does it feel like she's trying to convince herself of that?

"I missed it," she says, a harrumph in her voice, her frustration momentarily trumping the voice's intrusions. "The transition."

"There's always next time, my love," John says as he pops his door.

"Did you at least get your flyers handed out?" Maud waits for him to come around to her side and open hers. Not because she particularly wants to, but because something tells her she should. Part of her, a part driven by that little voice, moves to get up. To grab the handle. But something else tells her not to.

Why? the little voice in the back of her head nags, louder now. *You're a grown woman. You can open your car door on your own. What's next?*

"I did," John says as he comes around and opens her door. He occasionally takes trips outside Trinity Springs to spread flyers, to find potential candidates for the number of unoccupied homes in the community. And on special occasions, he allows Maud to accompany him It can get a little cooped up attending to the home all day, even when they have help.

As Maud steps out of the car, she looks up at that massive house where she and John live. It's an enormous colonial, with those tall, pretty columns in the front that remind her of a Roman temple. Tons of windows all around letting in natural light, and a fantastic placement at the end of the cul-de-sac.

Sometimes Maud thinks this house is a little much for just the two of them, but then she thinks about how, soon enough, she'll give John a child, hopefully a son, and they can start filling the place out a little more. Like all their other neighbors do.

Give him? the voice asks. *Is that it? Is it something you're going to give him?*

Yes, Maud thinks in her own voice. A child is a gift she's going to give her husband.

But the voice retaliates, cuts her to her core with something she knows, deep down, is true. *It's something he's going to take from you.*

"Sweetheart?"

Maud looks up at John, into his eyes, and for a moment she's frightened, but not in a way she understands at any more than a base, animalistic level. Like she's a house cat looking at a wild dog? No, that's not right, but it's something like that. But whatever it is, it's there and gone like déjà vu. Like a single bloody frame spliced into the romantic movie her life has become. But it leaves an impression. A burning thumbprint on her mind.

John asks, "Are you alright?", his eyes now back to their handsome normality.

"I...I feel..." Maud doesn't know how she feels, can't articulate it. Even though it's on the tip of her tongue. If she could just find it.

There has to be a way back, she thinks. *She* thinks. Not the voice. Not some intrusive thought. But Maud herself. A thought she recognizes as well and truly her own. But a way back to what? Why is her mind so scrambled?

"Who was that girl?" she asks, again using *girl*, not *woman*.

"The one at the diner?" John asks.

"Yes."

"That was your old girlfriend, Sorrel."

The way he uses girlfriend, it's the way Maud and the other gals of Trinity Springs use it—*I'm meeting my girlfriends for brunch. I'm playing bridge with my girlfriends.* The way women use it for women. But there's something about the word, something about the way men use it for women, that Maud thinks should be the right way. Was that it? Her old *girlfriend*? Was that the elation she felt when she thought of this woman?

"You remember her," John asks, "don't you?"

Maud thinks, tries to remember. Sorrel, yes. Maud remembers moving to Sorrel's town in the middle of the school year, being the new girl. She remembers Sorrel looking at her from across classrooms, looking skittish. When she finally introduced herself, Maud already knew who she was, had already been watching her, had already been interested in her.

"We went to school together," Maud says dreamily, like she's fishing for the answer John knows, and waiting for him to confirm or deny. "I think."

"You did indeed," he tells her, and Maud remembers herself and Sorrel cutting class one day, hanging out under the bleachers. That swelling feeling hits the bottom of her stomach again, and it feels like she's butted up against something she's tried to hide from herself. "Are you feeling alright?"

"I'm not sure," she says. She's wading in these Sorrel memories, feeling like there's something there to uncover, something she hasn't yet found but is oh-so-close to. "We went to school together," she says again, "but there's...something else..."

"Let's get you inside." John swoops her up, pulling her in close. He takes her into the kitchen and sets her down in a stool at the marble-topped island, gets her a glass of water. "Why don't you have something to eat?"

Maud nods. Yes, something to eat. That will make her feel better. She picks a peach up from the bowl on the table, lifts it to her lips. Yet another thing she loves about Trinity Springs; it seems like none of the food ever goes bad here, even if you leave it out. The reality is John's army of maids and cooks and cleaners, their work seen but themselves invisible. Just like the gardeners. They're always there to make sure everything is pristine.

"No, no, honey, not that." John takes the peach from her hand and pulls a Tupperware box out of the fridge. He pulls a sandwich from it, placing it on a small plate for her. "Try this instead," he says, setting it down. It's white bread, a large toothpick stabbed through it, lancing its meat, lettuce, and slice of tomato in place. Even the condiments, the mayo and single drip of spicy mustard, seem magically held still.

That déjà vu feeling happens to Maud again when John slides the plate towards her. It's like an electrical current, a memory of some kind. But a memory she can barely remember. Something that swims past her before she can get a good look at it. She thinks, *Oh, well*. If she forgot it so easily, it probably wasn't that important. She picks up the sandwich, hesitates. What kind of meat is this? It looks a little too juicy and fresh for how long it's supposedly been in the fridge. The bread is still perfect, like it's just come out of the breadbox, not soaked with the juices or the mayonnaise at all. She shrugs, guesses *the magic of Tupperware.*

"Could we invite Sorrel over for dinner?" Maud asks. The thought makes her disproportionately happy. She can't figure out why, though. Something's wrong. Why hasn't she heard that intrusive voice? Where did it go?

"I think that's a lovely idea," he says.

Spurned by a gesture from John, Maud bites into the sandwich. John stands above her, watching, making sure she eats the whole thing, and Maud forgets entirely about all those earlier uncomfortable feelings.

REPRESSION

Sorrel orders a line of shots and downs them all in a row. The bar's blasting rock music quickly recedes to a lull at the back of her head and warmth spreads throughout her limbs. The whiskey is a rush to the head and she feels a delightful tingle in her extremities. It's working. The night scene in a remote town like Beacon isn't much, but this place has alcohol and other dancing bodies, and that's all she needs to blast all those bad thoughts from her mind.

Sorrel had never been in a relationship before Maud. Not one that really counted. She'd had playground crushes, "gone out" with boys in a way that amounted to calling them her boyfriend and occasionally holding their hand on the playground.

But there had never been anything like Maud before.

Like love.

They had to keep it a secret because, for some reason Sorrel never really got a clear picture of, girls weren't supposed to go out with other girls.

"Fuck that," Maud said one evening when Sorrel mentioned it. They were sitting in the middle of the baseball field after school, lying down in the grass and watching the sun get lower and lower.

Sorrel understood then how she was drawn to Maud, wondered why it took her so long to think it was that she was jealous of her body. No, nothing as simple as that. Or maybe something much simpler? She wondered how she could've ever been so blind when, in the showers after gym class, Maud turned at the waist and looked right at her.

She takes another shot.

They had to keep it a secret, which was far easier for them than two boys in the same position, Sorrel guessed; people weren't so suspicious of two young girls spending so much time together, of being alone together. Sleepovers and even changing in front of one another. When Maud spent the night she did it in Sorrel's bed with their parents' permission, and for the longest time no one seemed any the wiser. In the dark, with the lights off, Sorrel felt Maud's fingers gently creep up her leg, felt Maud's lips on hers. That night they decided to devise a secret language, something only the two of them understood.

Another shot.

But it wasn't just arousal that made Sorrel gravitate towards Maud. Yes, a whole new sensory world had opened up for Sorrel; it was the first time she'd ever been with anyone outside of a few stray kisses. But she knew she loved Maud when she saw the way she interacted with the world. She moved through it carefree, but not ignorantly. She was herself already, and so young, and Sorrel envied that, loved Maud for that as much as she did for opening her heart to the possibility that love could come to her in the form of a woman.

She downs the last shot.

There's a voice in her head, one she's been conscious of, one she's heard many times before, telling her this is a bad idea. Occasionally, like tonight, the voice uses therapy language to make itself sound more official, tells her this is a poor coping mechanism. That she's avoiding confronting her feelings. That she's engaging in self-sabotage yet again. She knows all this to be true. Normally she listens to that voice.

But not tonight.

Tonight Sorrel needs a very special, very specific thing, and she's decided the only thing that can give it to her is the exact behavior that voice wants to avoid. What she really needs is the memories of today gone, blasted out of her mind, the sight of Maud ripped from her brain. But since she can't actually pull that memory out, she decides she'll bury it instead. Under alcohol and sweat and adrenaline and hopefully sex.

She'll deal with it tomorrow. If she deals with it at all.

Sorrel orders another line of shots and downs them all, but has enough wherewithal to intersperse the whiskey with water. It's the last sensible decision she'll make tonight. She wades out into the mediocre dance floor, following her instincts, feelings, muscle memory. They all drag her away from the slowly-encroaching army of disparate men, roving predators searching for the night's prey, and to the center of the dancers. She surrounds herself with fellow women, inserting herself into a group that accepts her without hesitation, the unspoken language of women protecting one of their own.

Sorrel sways and moves, at first aggressively, as if she can shake and twist and gyrate those memories, and even the feeling of them, right out of her body. It doesn't work. But what does work to help bury them is when one of those women from the group moves closer to her. Her aesthetic is punk; tattoos on her arms and a small hoop in her nose. Combat boots, the side of her head shaved, the rest of her hair neon pink. The pink-haired woman's hands move exploratorily with the music, which, as if on cue, changes to something just a little slower.

The woman comes closer to Sorrel, her hands on her hips, and Sorrel realizes her own arms are around the woman's shoulders, that they're getting closer. Something swells in the pit of Sorrel's stomach, a sensation that feels like it's going to lift her up and carry her away. She feels like she's approaching a ledge she can't un-jump from, the same feeling she used to have around Maud, and suddenly the feeling in her stomach rises. It's not a pleasant sensation anymore, but one she's far too familiar with.

Vomit.

Sorrel makes it off the dance floor at least, no idea what happened to the punk girl or how she might feel about her sudden bolting. Her hand's covering her mouth, every mixed drink she's had throughout the night, half-digested pomegranate seeds, and microwaved chicken strips from the back of her freezer spewing out from between her fingers as she shoulders her way into the ladies room to get so sick in the handicapped stall that her eyes burn and she blacks out for a moment.

Sorrel's awake later. She's not sure how much later. It feels like only a moment. Was she even unconscious? She's not on the floor of the bathroom. Not entirely anyway. Just crouched in the corner of the stall. The toilet is a ruined mess, a lump of something she can't identify in the middle of her pool of vomit. The way her chest feels, it might as well be her heard.

Christ, girl, the fuck is wrong with you? It's the same voice in her head speaking. Even it's fed up. But she can't afford to listen to it now. Those memories are coming back and she can't let them. Sorrel stands up, washes her face and her mouth and some of her hair in the bathroom sink, silently apologizing to the janitor and whatever poor soul tries to use the handicapped stall next.

When she goes back out to the dance floor, she spots the lights shining off the same girl's pink hair. She's dancing in the same group of girls as before, but Sorrel doesn't return to them. She can't. She pushes down more than her memories of Maud and approaches the bar. She asks for a ginger ale to pretend there's whiskey in it, and waits for one of those skulking predators, the dozens of interchangeable men from the bar, to approach her.

THE DOUBLE

There is Sorrel, and then there is someone else. Someone watching her from across the room. This person sees Sorrel return from the bathroom to swing wide around the dance floor and the woman with the pink hair, sees her go back to the bar, sees a man approach her. This watcher sees a standard courtship ritual begin, one she's aware of, despite never having actually lived it herself. This someone else watches the man and Sorrel, watches them leave together, and knows what is going to happen, what they are going to do. And, more importantly, what Sorrel is going to *not* do. What she is going to repress. To swallow.

As Sorrel leaves, she looks over her shoulder, like something bothers her. She looks in the direction of the watcher, but if she sees her, she either brushes it off, or is simply too drunk to care. She leaves the bar with the man, and fucks him in the backseat of an obnoxiously-large pickup truck. At least there's leg room.

But any bystander, any bargoer who wasn't really paying attention to their surroundings, would have thought the mixed-race woman with the long, curly hair had stayed in the bar. Because there she was. Sorrel. Or at least someone who looks just like her. Standing on the edge of the dance floor, occluded in shadow. Despite having supposedly just left with someone.

This woman who looks exactly like Sorrel has her hair done differently, wears it down, curls shielding her ears, tickling her shoulders. She wears a buttoned coat instead of the tight jeans and boots Sorrel had on when she entered the bar. In the dark, it was impossible to see her feet were bare. This woman may look just like her, but she is someone different. Someone new. Another presence suddenly and violently pushed into the world when Sorrel blacked out, expelling what she thought was only vomit in the handicap stall of the ladies' restroom.

The double, this other Sorrel, wreathed in a coat stolen from over the wall of the bathroom stall, its original owner too drunk to notice it missing, looks out across the bar. It's loud and scary, but aren't everyone's first few moments in the world?

She quickly accustoms herself to the sound, to the world itself, in a way that Sorrel—that any other human—could never. Some physiological feat she doesn't understand. Nor does she need to. In fact, she only understands one thing, a desire deep in the bottom of her belly.

The girl with the pink hair.

She's still on the dance floor, still dancing within that protective circle of women, all of them moving together. This second Sorrel moves forward on wobbly feet that quickly steady the closer she gets.

When the woman with the pink hair sees the second Sorrel approach her, her whole attitude changes. She smiles brighter, dances closer.

"I didn't think you were coming back," she says into the double's ear once they're intertwined with one another again. Is it *again*? Has she ever done this before, really?

"Sorry," the double says, "I'm here." Deep down she knows, somehow, that she won't be for long. That her time on this world is limited. That, soon, she will return, repressed, to somewhere in the deep pit of the true Sorrel's mind. Physically reduced to little more than the slick puddle of goop she was born as. She tries not to imagine what her other half is doing right now, how she's trying to keep the demons of her own desire at bay. Instead, the double, the repressed Sorrel made manifest, does what she wants, what she needs, and pulls the woman with the pink hair closer, kisses her in front of God and everyone.

For once unashamed.

part 2

Apértif

THE INVITATION

Sorrel sits in her car in front of 7780 Dixon Street, right in the middle of one of the dumbest decisions she's ever made. She's still hungover from last night, still covered in sweat and hastily-applied perfume. Big, dark sunglasses hide the face she's so reluctant to look into the mirror at. She imagines running makeup and dark circles under her eyes. She hasn't showered since last night, only gave herself a quick wipe down after the guy from last night—*Bobby? Rick? The hell was his name? Does it matter if I'll never see him again?*—finished up. She'd rolled out of his bed as soon as he'd started snoring and staggered back to her apartment.

Where she found the invitation.

And now here she is, sitting in her car in front of an unknown house on an unknown street in an unknown neighborhood far too goddamn early in the morning. The only thing that's keeping her from getting sick is the sound and smell of Burke Lake somewhere off to her right. The brackish water evens her out in a way the medicine didn't, tethers her to the world when her body wants to shut down. Go back to sleep. Forget everything from the last twenty-four hours like it was all some awful nightmare.

And part of her thinks it was. She has some strange memory of glimpsing herself in the crowd at the bar. Another Sorrel with another set of clothes and something different in her eyes, a spark, a life in her that she hasn't felt for quite some time. Such a sight wasn't that far afield from her normal drunken dreams; intense and strange. But it was all a dream. And maybe if that second Sorrel was a dream, seeing Maud was too.

But the invitation in her hands is real.

Sorrel remembers picking something off her door when she got home last night, but only barely remembers it was this. She rubs the thick paper between her fingers, looks at the fancy letters all done up in (Maud's?) calligraphy. You are cordially invited. Like it's a formal event.

7780 Dixon Street.

From her car Sorrel can see the building's door, the polished, white wood without a speck of dust on it. The ornate, brass knocker in the shape of an apple.

She's in front of the door before she even realizes she's out of the car. Grabs the handle. Yanks it open. Looks down a long, dark hallway, flanked on either side by red floor-length curtains and lit by lamps dangling from the ceiling, an L-bend at the far end. It looks like a throat, some massive, yawning maw welcoming her inside.

But even this obvious nefariousness is not enough to deter her. Maybe because she's still a little drunk. Either way she needs to know. Seeing Maud yesterday, it lit a fire inside her, a fire she thought withered and died when Maud was taken away from her. It's begun to spark again, to grow and breathe, and this is the only way she can think to feed it. To follow her. To find her.

She steps forward, and the hallway swallows her.

BELLY OF THE BEAST

WHAT ARE YOU DOING? Sorrel asks herself as she steps into this strange house on this strange street in this strange neighborhood. *Why are you doing this? You're going to get yourself killed.* But she thinks about Maud, about her face, how standing outside the diner she was smiling with everything but her eyes, how terrified and fearful those eyes looked.

You're doing this for her, Sorrel tells herself. *To get her back.* That's motivation enough to get her to do anything in the world.

She steps into the house.

There's a record playing somewhere ahead of her. Soft, jazzy music. Like a dentist's waiting room in a decade gone by. Sorrel follows it. There's only one way to go, after all; through the canyon of red curtains, toward the bend. She listens to the sounds her soft-soled boots make on the tile floor; practically nothing, the curtains swallowing up even the thought of an echo.

Don't run. You don't know what's around that corner.

She doesn't run, but she does hurry, especially when she's in the middle dark, a spot in the hall where light from neither of the dangling lamps properly reaches. Passing through that spot of lesser light, Sorrel nearly stumbles, reaches out to grab the curtains for balance, but thinks better of it.

Touch nothing in this place.

Instead she widens her feet, stretches her arms out to either side for balance. She hurries through the pool of dark, but even after she gets out, there's something fuzzy in her head. Like a dizziness, an inner ear thing, but even that's not quite right. It's like a sudden vertigo, or even a contact high. Like there's something constantly being pumped into the air in this house.

Keep going.

She doesn't know how to explain it, but she feels like her answers are right around that L-bend. Sorrel pushes through the dark spot as fast as she can. The whole time nervous, paranoid, feeling like there are eyes looking out at her from the dark, hands ready to reach out and grab her. Perhaps, she thinks, that is simply the existence she's been trained to expect.

But she can't take the chance. She pushes through, takes the turn in the hall, and after about ten more feet, finds herself in a large room. This one, too, is covered in those floor-to-ceiling curtains. The only other egress is a door on the other end of the room, a door with a handle in its center. There may be other doors or even windows behind the curtains, but if there are, Sorrel can't see them. The white tile is the same, and there are easy chairs and small side-tables that hold bouquets of flowers and trays of coffee cups gathered in clusters around the room.

The *waiting* room.

Because that's what it is, Sorrel thinks. That's exactly what it is. It looks like she's going to sit down and wait for a dentist.

And just like any waiting room, there's a receptionist desk. Behind it sits a woman who looks like she's in the wrong decade; hot red lipstick, cat's-eye eyeglasses, the same kind of other-the-shoulder sweater Maud was wearing, clasped together at the neck. Even her bra seems to be dated, Sorrel notices, the woman's breasts appearing pointed and missile-like, like the sweater girls from the '50s. It makes her nametag, reading KATE, slump a little to the side.

Pay attention, Sorrel suddenly tells herself, and when she tears her eyes away from the woman she also notices the dated switchboard peeking out from the red curtains behind her.

Kate jumps in her seat when she suddenly notices Sorrel, turns and closes the curtains so the switchboard is out of view.

"Good evening!" She quickly composes herself, shuffling papers in front of her. It's like Sorrel's presence is a test she could quite possibly be reprimanded for failing. She picks up a pencil from the desk. "My name's Kate. You must be Sorrel." The woman's tongue parts her lips and she touches the pencil tip to it, ready to proceed.

"Um..." How did this woman know who she was? *The invitation.* "Yeah. Do you know a woman named Maud Jacobson?"

Kate's brow furrows and Sorrel can see the flash of recognition across her face. "Maud Jacob—Oh, honey, you must mean Maud *Kelly*. Mr. Kelly's new bride!"

Kelly. John Kelly. So that's the man's name. John Kelly of Trinity Springs. Sorrel has a name and a town now. That may very well be all she needs.

"Of course I know her, silly. Mr. Kelly's practically the mayor here. And she's the one who invited you. We're familiar. Gal pals." She blushes a little at *gal pals*. "We've seen each other at the mixers and such. Great bridge player. I'm sorry, I'm just chattering away. A chatty Kathy! Well, Chatty Kate." She laughs at her own joke while Sorrel stares. Is the woman's mouth just a little too big for her face? "Anyway, Mr. Kelly said that when you got here, you could come right on in. You can follow me." Kate stands, tiptoes in her high heels out behind the desk, and for the first time Sorrel gets a look at all of her. She's short. Even in those heels she's about a head shorter than Sorrel. Her thighs are covered in a polka-dot skirt, her calves nylon stockings, the kind with that strip going up the back of her calves.

What is this Sorrel's feeling?

You know what it is. It's the same thing that got you in trouble with Maud. Stop it.

A flurry of images Sorrel quickly represses; her walking up to Kate. Coming closer and closer. Kate backing away until she's in a corner, pretending to be timid, but the look in her eyes really pleading. Nowhere left to go, just like a game Sorrel and Maud used to play. Sorrel standing above her. Kate looking up into her eyes, pleading not just for it to happen, but for the anticipation to last longer. Their mouths are dry, their bodies warm. She's ripping those stockings right off Kate's legs like a predator going for the most tender part of her.

Stop. She pushes those desires down. *You remember what happened the last time you thought things like this.*

"You're very lucky," Kate says, pulling Sorrel back to the moment. "People can't come into Trinity Springs unless they're invited." She leads Sorrel across the room to the only other visible door, the one with its handle in the center. "Most women have to wait quite some time before Mr. Kelly will see them."

Women. She said *women.* Not *people.* Who the hell is this man? What is this place?

Kate takes the door by the handle, but before she can turn it, Sorrel reaches out and touches her elbow. The questions come too fast for Kate to understand them. Or for Sorrel to really filter them, blurring into nonsensical words: "What is this place? What's going on here? *Whoishe*?"

Kate glances down, sees Sorrel's hand on her.

And then Kate takes a large, visible step back. Her heels clack against the tile much louder than they should, punctuating her movement.

Sorrel can see something in her eyes then. It's something bright and helpless. For a moment Sorrel thinks it's like the thing she just fantasized about, the anticipation anxiety, the play-fear she imagined in Kate's face, what she remembers feeling herself when Maud approached her. That fear of the forbidden, finding out you don't just want something, don't just desire it, but *need* it, only for it to be denied to you. Does Kate want Sorrel to stand above her, to back her into a corner, to stand there as she shreds the nylons off her legs, but know it's something that can never happen? What Sorrel sees in her eyes, she doesn't know if she's projecting, but it looks like the way she imagined herself to look when Maud first touched her: mouth slightly agape, brows furrowed, hands by her stomach. A look that said *Is this real? Is this a possibility? Are we allowed to have this?*

But she looks deeper, stops projecting, and realizes Sorrel has never seen anyone this afraid before. Truly afraid. Even Maud. Even herself in the mirror. Even when their childhood tryst was outed.

Kate suddenly steps closer. So close that Sorrel reverts for a moment, thinks she's about to kiss her. But the look in Kate's eyes is frantic, not passionate. Desperate, but not longing. "Don't go outside," Kate whispers conspiratorially. Like there's someone lurking, listening, right behind the curtains and she can't afford to be heard. "Don't go outside after sundown. Not *you*. Not in this town."

A chill runs through Sorrel. She can feel goosebumps on her arms. She suddenly feels like the powerless one. And not in a good way.

"What...did you just say to me?"

Kate swallows, and Sorrel can actually see the lump in her throat.

"Trust me. Please. Just don't go outside after sundown."

In the next instant, Kate composes herself like it never happened. Like her little outburst was someone else entirely. Or didn't happen at all. She stands up straighter. Clears her throat. Looks at the door.

After sundown. That's what she'd said. Not *dark.* But *after sundown.* For Sorrel, there's a horrible recognition in those words, a fear that's come out of left field. She'd been so afraid what the world would do because of the part of her that loved Maud, she completely forgot about the other aspects of herself.

"Mr. Kelly is waiting for you," Kate says, gesturing, taking another quick half-step back, silently telling Sorrel, *Go on. We're done here,* and Sorrel sees the fear is gone entirely, wiped from Kate, and knows she won't be able to drag it out of her. At least not now. Sorrel recognizes that body language, how closed-off Kate has become. If there was a moment to pry it out of her, that moment is gone. She wonders if Kate is even aware of her outburst or if it came from some unknown corner of her core.

Sorrel takes the handle of the door and pushes it open.

Sunlight strikes her with a beam far brighter than it was when she first went into the waiting room, and when her eyes finally adjust and she takes in the bright, wide suburban street she's inexplicably found herself on, he's there. Right there. That man and that car sitting at the curb.

John Kelly, leaning against the hood of that '50s convertible, smiling at Sorrel like he's happy to see an old friend. The Cary Grant type. So handsome. So charming. In another world, another time, maybe Sorrel could have fallen for someone like this. Maybe fallen for him specifically, with his broad shoulders and dark eyes, that bright orange flower on his lapel. A man out of time. So out of time that where he came from, their union might be illegal, one where Sorrel might have to try and pass.

What have you done? What are you doing? What is this spell? What is this place?

Maud is nowhere to be seen.

"Sorrel," John says with a smile that would have fooled anyone else. "Glad to see you could make it." For a moment she thinks he's going to offer her a hand, a hand she knows she should never take. But he doesn't. He walks along the side of the car and opens the door for her. "Maud will be so thrilled you're here. You absolutely *must* join us for dinner."

TRINITY SPRINGS

Sorrel keeps herself ready, knows her plan of attack; if he comes at her, she'll raise her left arm and block him as much as she can. Then her right will be free to hit back. Go for the sensitive areas; eyes, ears, nose. The crotch is probably not so useful here, not if she doesn't have a clear shot. Hit him hard, then jump out of the car. Don't worry about actually opening the door. Just jump out of the convertible and haul ass. She knows she's going to need to have movement available to her, hasn't buckled in. If he's noticed, he hasn't said anything about it.

But that violent scenario doesn't come to pass. John just drives the car, whistling to himself. It's a soft tune that has a couple sharp high notes Sorrel can't place. Despite his cheery exterior, Sorrel never takes her eyes off him, never letting him leave her peripheral, only looking past him or around him to get a sense of where they are.

A terrible, warped sense.

Brilliant, white houses, perfectly-manicured lawns, American flags flapping in the breeze, people out in the street waving at the car as they pass by. The sky is that so-perfect-it-almost-looks-fake, like a movie backdrop. Sorrel can smell barbecues and freshly-cut grass and lawn sprinklers. There's something else, though, some sickly-sweet smell underneath it all whose source she can't identify. It reminds her of roadkill roasting on a summer blacktop.

Sorrel tries to hide holding her breath and instead looks out past John into the neighborhood, trying to avoid the way the roadkill smell makes her feel woozy, gripping the armrests. Almost every yard has someone in it; children playing in driveways, men grilling or washing their cars, women gardening, or sunbathing in modest one-piece swimsuits. It doesn't escape Sorrel's notice that every single one of those families is white. It's the kind of thing she expected out of this place, this man. The only brown people she sees at all are workers unloading lawn care machines from a large trailer. Weedwhackers and leaf blowers and ride-on mowers. Each one of them stops what they're doing, momentarily pauses as John's car trundles by, and Sorrel swears the workers all look at her, not him. There's a sadness in their eyes she can't quite place.

But what makes even less sense is where this neighborhood is, geographically. Sorrel tries to measure it in her mind, how deep she went into that house, the winding path she took and where she should be. She's only lived in Beacon for a few years, isn't super familiar with the Gough's Cove neighborhood, but she still knows this place being here isn't right. They should be out in the middle of the lake to the north of the town by now. Not to mention that there simply isn't an upper-class gated community like this anygoddamnwhere near Beacon. Sorrel is an introvert, but she's not a recluse. There's no way she simply wouldn't know this place was here.

"Where are we?" she asks, plain and simple.

"Trinity Springs," John says, waving his hand at the neighborhood. As if it's obvious, like it answers everything. Sorrel hears a sudden scream, but it reorients itself in her mind to a shriek of childlike delight.

"What is Trinity Springs?"

"It's my home," he says, looking around, taking it all in as if he's doing it for the first time in a long time. "*Our* home."

Sorrel looks up at the sky. It looks strange in a way she can't entirely place, like the blue is what's moving and the clouds are standing still. A shimmer moves across it like the surface of the water. Like the blue is a sheet hanging there and the wind is pushing against it.

What the fuck?

They drive on in silence for another moment, and Sorrel takes her phone out right in front of John. She doesn't hide it, wants him to know she has a potential weapon, a tool in her possession. She brings up her location app, but the buffering wheel just keeps spinning endlessly. A rarely-seen message in the top-left corner alerts her to the fact that she has NO SER-VICE.

What the hell is this place?

"This is more of a landline town, sweetheart," John says with a snicker. When Sorrel looks at him, he's smiling as if to say *gotcha!*, like he knew she was going to try that very move and was awaiting the chance to use that well-rehearsed line.

Cringing at being called sweetheart, Sorrel puts the phone back in her pocket, and decides she needs to be the one asking questions, the one on the offensive. She can't let him hold even a conversational advantage over her.

"So you're Maud's husband, huh?" None of it adds up in any conceivable way. Sure, people change when they grow out of teenagerdom, but did they change *this* much? The Maud she knew skipped just enough class to get a passing grade. The Maud she knew climbed up the tree behind Sorrel's house to sneak into her room. The Maud she knew spray-painted dicks on cop cars. Was she now part of some kind of cult or something? Could that explain her changes, this place?

"Yes, yes," John says, taking the car slowly, easily, throughout the neighborhood. "I'm her old man." He raises his left hand, holding out his ring finger. It's a simple, gold band. Very classic. Very traditional. Something about its plainness makes Sorrel angry.

She wants to ask him a million and one questions, but she restrains herself, knows not to overextend like she did with Kate. She doesn't get the same impression that she could spook John like she spooked Kate, but she still knows she needs to play this smarter.

She needs to gather more information before she starts to make herself look desperate for anything.

Instead, she asks a simple question, "Maud invited me for dinner?"

"She did indeed. And we'd better hurry up and get inside before the sun goes down. It can be dangerous for someone...*like you* to be out on the street after dark."

A slithering icicle colder than anything Sorrel ever felt slid down her back. There it was, the veiled threat she'd been waiting for. She doesn't take her eyes off expressionless John, but thinks back to what she's already seen—the Americana, the white families, the dated cars and clothes. Is he implying the dark isn't safe for her because she's a woman, or because she's brown? Or because she's gay? Is he just absentmindedly threatening her as any man would, without thinking, or does he know exactly what he's threatening her with? Was Sorrel too busy watching him to notice an impossible, out-of-time, black-and-yellow sign posted somewhere along the way?

Is it even a threat? Is he looking out for me? Sorrel mentally scolds herself for slipping into the man-saves-woman mindset. It was so easy going there, just like how she'd gone to falling for John when she first laid eyes on him. *Jesus, what have you gotten yourself into?*

John is silent as he turns the car onto a different street. For the first time, Sorrel catches the name, the signpost thankfully passing by behind him. Bender Circle. John Kelly. Trinity Springs. Bender

Circle. A name, a town, a street. Though Sorrel isn't quite sure how much any of that matters anymore, considering this town shouldn't even be here. But regardless, it's a circle, a cul-de-sac. So wherever they're going, they're almost there. Just a few seconds later, John pulls the car into a driveway.

"Home again, home again, jiggety-jig." He looks Sorrel quickly up and down. "I'm sure Maud has a change of clothes in your size for dinner." He gets up and out, and for the first time Sorrel really looks around at this impossible place, at the house they've stopped in front of. She doesn't know houses by their types, just knows this one is huge. It's got those columns out front that remind her of ancient Roman architecture. A thousand windows looking out onto the street. A wraparound porch. An American flag high on a pole sprouting out of the flower bed. The yard is huge and well-manicured, has those telltale back-and-forth lines like a lawnmower has been through it only minutes ago.

Sorrel quickly glances at the other houses. They're all of a similar kind, like they were poured from the same mold. But it seems like John's house is just slightly larger. Almost imperceptibly-so. Is that deliberate?

"Are you coming?"

Sorrel turns, realizes she hasn't even gotten out of the car yet. John is standing by her door, holding it open for her. A small piece of Sorrel, the only part of her that isn't constantly on guard, thinks, *What a gentleman.* The rest of her thinks, *What are you thinking?*

Don't trust him. Don't trust anything you see. At least not until she gets to Maud. *And maybe not even then?*

John says, "Remember what I said about when the sun goes down." He doesn't say it like it's meant to be a threat, but a helpful reminder. Like he's looking out for her. *Be careful, sweetheart.*

Sorrel steps out of the car, into the driveway, not thanking John exactly, just giving him a curt nod. She looks over his shoulder at the sun, wonders how long it'll be, exactly, until it's down. When she walked into the waiting room it was mid-afternoon, but she doesn't get the sense that means anything here.

John shuts the car door behind her, says, "Welcome to my home," waving an arm at the enormous house. Just as he does, as if she were standing behind the front door waiting for a cue, Maud appears. She looks the same as before, as Sorrel saw her yesterday, dressed like a housewife from a particularly rose-colored decade gone by. Today she's wearing a sleeveless, floral sundress. Sorrel swallows the sudden lump in her throat that appears when she sees Maud's bare arms. Maud is already taller than Sorrel, and she stands even taller now in immaculately-white high heels, looking even taller on the house's porch. The image reminds Sorrel of one of the first times they were ever alone together, a stolen moment shifting from one classroom to the next. Sorrel still getting all her bags and books together, Maud standing next to her desk.

Hurry up, Maud said gently, and Sorrel was trying. Flustered. Nervous. Angry because she could never figure out why she was so flustered and nervous in front of this girl. Maud reached out then, and without warning grabbed a handful of Sorrel's curly hair. Pulled her head back. Sorrel could feel the tug on her scalp, feel the way her back arched as she tried to follow the direction Maud was taking her. She noticed how her movement pushed her breasts out, how her feet widened but her knees stayed together. Her head pulled all the way back, she looked up into Maud's face. The wind was taken out of her. She knew then.

Hurry. Up, Maud said again, this time with a devilish little smile lifting the right side of her mouth, the first glimpse of the little games they liked to play with one another.

Yes, Sorrel had said, as much a response to Maud as an acknowledgement of what she truly felt. *Yes, yes.*

"Sorrel, honey!" Maud takes to her tiptoes and waves at Sorrel as if she's trying to stand out from a crowd. "I'm so glad you could make it!" She comes down from the porch, hurrying down the drive, and throws her arms around Sorrel. It's a feeling she hasn't felt in years. The pure and utter bliss. The sense of safety. Of nostalgia. She lifts her own arms and hugs Maud back, longing for the feel of her skin once again.

You feel just like I remember.

The hug ends far too quickly, Maud pulling away, looking Sorrel up and down, Sorrel's hands still outstretched, as if she can draw Maud back into her arms.

"It's been too long."

It really has. But all Sorrel can do is nod. She feels like if she speaks, everything will come spilling out, and she needs to remain composed. To wait. To reconnoiter.

"Why don't you come inside? Our chef's working on dinner, and I can have her whip us up a couple cocktails before we eat."

Maud grabs Sorrel by the elbow, her grip tight, and it feels so much like the way Maud used to grab her, used to hold her, that Sorrel melts, can do nothing but follow along as Maud pulls her up the drive, into the house. When John shuts the front door behind them, it's louder than it should be, feels like a curtain closing, cutting off a part of the world Sorrel can never go back to again.

KATE

Katherine Anderson, Kate to all her friends, watches the young woman, Sorrel, leave the waiting room, knowing with certainty that she will never see her again. Knowing that, in all likelihood, no one will ever see her again. At least not after tonight. With that weight around her shoulders, Kate closes up the waiting room like she normally would. When Mr. Kelly told her to watch the waiting room that morning, he said that a woman named Sorrel Washington would be arriving later. After her, Kate was free to close up. No one else would be crossing the border into Trinity Springs. And so, obediently, Kate closes up the waiting room in the way she's used to—shutting and locking the front door, pulling the crimson curtains closed, and leaving through the same door Sorrel left through.

But when Kate emerges into the outside world, she's in a different place from where she knows Sorrel ended up. Not dramatically so, but it isn't a suburban sidewalk. There's no handsome man waiting for her. Instead, Kate finds herself in a small parking lot, her little blue roadster its only occupant.

"

Her stomach growls angrily, uncomfortably, as if it knows she can head home now and eat. But she can't; she has to stay on her diet, has to slim down for Gary. Both he and her neighbors made a couple offhand comments about her weight in the past couple weeks. Nothing major, just that she was looking *full*, or *plump*, but she knew what those words really meant. She was beginning to take the shape of the kind of person who wasn't wanted in Trinity Springs. And if she wasn't wanted, she could always be forced to leave. Gary wouldn't be the first husband who'd traded up. Maybe she'd just have a couple slices of bread when she got home. Just enough to stave off her growling stomach.

Halfway across the lot, heels clicking against the asphalt, Kate turns around and looks at the building behind her. Its plain brick facade, completely absent any sign detailing what it is or what it does. There are windows, but in the bizarre logic of Trinity Springs that she has somehow gotten used to over the years (how long has it been, really?), they're only decorative; she has never seen a window on the inside of that building. Only those waterfalling red curtains.

Kate gets into her car, slides her bags across the roadster's bench seat, but before she goes anywhere, before she puts the key in the ignition, she closes her eyes and listens to the sounds of the nearby river. It circles all of Trinity Springs, a protective natural border around town, turning the neighborhood into its own little island. Sometimes, on days like today, days when she's forced to do something she doesn't want to, doesn't want to even think about,

Kate daydreams about how easy it would be, how no one would notice if she just took her car over the little truss bridge to the north and left Trinity Springs behind her once and for all.

People have done it before, she thinks, her head subconsciously turning in that direction. Every few years there's a runaway, someone who thinks they can make it across the bridge or—God forbid—through the river itself. It was often wives, occasionally the workers in Trinity Springs; the gardeners and landscapers, personal chefs and maids. The people who lived on the outskirts of town, not in the palatial houses, but in cramped apartment blocks, shielded from the sight of Trinity Springs proper by half a mile of woods. All people who were brought here against their will, whether they knew it or not. People who were brought here to serve others.

Like she was.

Often upon an escape attempt, Kate and the other wives would gossip about who tried it, the reason why, when seeing one another at the grocery store or social clubs. Not at their jobs. Never their jobs. None of them had any jobs besides attending to their households.

Did you hear Gertrude tried to leave? She tried to make it across the river.

No one ever made it across the river.

Those runaway wives would often be seen placed back in their homes later, the dark-skinned men and women working the gardens and kitchens again as well. Whenever any of them returned, they always had that same glassy-eyed ten-mile stare. And when they didn't return, someone else simply took their place. Sometimes Kate would wonder what could possess someone to do something like that. Leave Trinity Springs? After they all fought so hard to get here? After they all gave up so much? Kate remembers how she got here, remembers her husband Gary coming home from the bar one night talking about a guy he met, a realtor or something, he said. He had the guy's card, but it was weird. It just said his name, John Kelly, and had a small graphic of two closed wrought-iron gates. He told Gary all about this beautiful neighborhood, a new gated community that was just beginning construction. Perfect timing, Gary said, because they were just looking to move. Their own neighborhood was becoming unsettling, he always said, with all these new people moving in from out of the city. And unsettling was one step away from dangerous.

Trinity Springs, on the other hand, isn't dangerous at all. There is no police force, because there is no crime. Only a neighborhood watch, everyone looking out for one another. Everyone watching one another. A gated community, its residents are carefully hand-filtered by John Kelly himself to leave no room for undesirables. Would anyone, Kate, any of the wives in the neighborhood, want to throw that all away?

Most days the concept seemed unfathomable.

But for some reason not today. Leaving Trinity Springs doesn't seem so unfathomable as she's sitting there in her car, and she sees a dark-skinned man, his head hanging low, weedwhacking the edges of a nearby lawn to perfection. The man looks up momentarily, seems to realize who is sitting in Kate's car, and suddenly averts his eyes. Leaving doesn't seem so insane when she remembers the sight of Sorrel Washington walking through that door, John Kelly on the other side. Kate thinks she'd rather have seen someone go into a wood chipper. It may have been less traumatizing.

Her stomach growls, as if to remind her that this is where she belongs. This is where she must stay.

Kate pulls away from the building, from that place where she sentenced another woman to death without her knowledge, eager to leave all those uncomfortable sensations behind. Kate doesn't man the waiting room often, maybe once every few months, when John Kelly expects a new resident, but the routine has been drilled into her.

She follows another routine as she leaves the building, heads home and finds her neighbor, Geraldine Wedge, watering the garden. Geraldine waves as Kate gets out of the car, and Kate waves back. Geraldine hesitates for a moment, and then asks, "Coming from work, hun?"

"Yes," Kate says. Quietly. Passively. A clear indicator to Geraldine that she does not want to talk about it. And Geraldine acquiesces. She knows. All the women know. Kate sees Geraldine's smile fade only momentarily, like a skip on a record, before she returns to her chipper self. But it's there, the knowledge between the two of them. Festering.

Another one. Another woman is here. But for how long?

Kate leaves Geraldine to her flowers and goes inside. As is expected of her, she changes into a different outfit, and for a moment while she changes is spared the physical pain of constant female presentableness; she flexes her bare toes in the fluff of her bedroom carpet, glad to be free of the arc of high heels and the constant fight of keeping the line on the backs of her stockings straight. She takes off her bra, feels the cool air conditioning against her skin. She removes a few pins from her hair, realizes how hard it's been tugging on her scalp all day.

Kate isn't sure if the moment of peace is worth the hassle of changing into something entirely new. No, she knows it isn't. It's relaxation, comfort, dangled in front of her before it's yanked away just as fast.

She suddenly feels sick with something far beyond bile.

Oh, no. Oh, no, please, not now!

This has happened before.

And it will happen again.

Kate knows what it is, and she knows *why* it is. It's happening because she spent so long lingering on the past, on the possibilities, on where she came from and how she got there. Because she spent so long thinking about Trinity Springs, and the possibility of rejecting it. Because she spent so long without food from this place, but especially meat, fasting as she was to try to appear thin for Gary. Something she spent so long shoving deep down inside her is rising up, trying to get free.

But she has things to do, so she pushes down the pain.

But the pain pushes back. It's beyond physical, and it's coming, whether she likes it or not. Lava comes rushing up her esophagus and Kate makes it to the bathroom but not the toilet, closing her eyes as the bile breaches her throat, stings her tonsils, burns the back of her nose. It feels so much worse than simple vomit. For a moment, her whole world is the eye-watering, putrid stink of what she throws up into the bathroom sink, what she knows she'll have to dispose of later in the most grisly fashion that is the price of admission into Trinity Springs.

And then she hears Gary's car in the driveway.

She darts out of the bathroom, into the bedroom, makes herself presentable and hustles into the living room just as Gary walks through the front door. Like it's all planned, all staged. Kate can hear the audience's canned sighs of relief as she walks into the living room. *Phew, she made it!*

Gary greets her, she's sure, but she isn't really paying attention. If he does, it is something cursory, something sapped of true interest or curiosity. How was her day? Well, she probably killed another girl by bringing her into this place, so there's that. Maybe poor Sorrel is dying even as Gary sits at the kitchen table and eats his meatloaf without even really acknowledging Kate. Maybe she's being ripped to pieces as he plops himself down in front of the television and Kate brings him another beer. Maybe her blood is congealing in John Kelly's basement as Kate reads the lecherous look in Gary's eyes later that evening.

When he pulls her into the bedroom, he doesn't strip her naked, which she realizes she's happy for. Nor does he expect her mouth. He just stands before her and waits, his pants unbuttoned but not unzipped, like she's supposed to read his mind and know what he wants. She slips her panties out from under her skirt which seems to send a bright green *go* light directly into Gary's brain. He twirls her around and bends her over the bed, is inside her without any foreplay, and Kate is more bored than anything else. She is only marginally aware of her body as Gary grunts behind her, untucks her shirt and pushes her still-hooked bra up her torso so he can access her breasts.

Instead, she's wondering if there's still time to undo what she's done. What time is it now? How long has Sorrel been alone with John? But if she somehow told Sorrel to go back, if she somehow listened, and leaving somehow worked, what would happen to Kate? What would happen to the other wives in town? The workers? None of whom are there of their own free will. She fantasizes, separate from her body, about each and every one of them walking out. Could they do it? There weren't enough husbands to stop them if they did. And what would happen if they tried? Would the husbands resort to violence?

A warm, wet glob of something hits the small of her back, and Kate sighs with relief that Gary is finished with her—it didn't take long, it never does. She sighs and rolls her eyes with expected annoyance that, once again, she will have to take care of herself in the dark and the quiet as he sleeps.

Then she tenses with confusion.

Because she can still feel his hands holding her hips. Even tighter now. She can still feel him inside her, suddenly inexplicably softer, far softer than he ever is immediately after finishing.

Kate looks over her shoulder and sees Gary's head bent backwards and there's a crimson curtain draping down his neck and chest, a bloody waterfall that's cresting across the small of Kate's back and buttocks even now. She screams, trying to get away, but Gary is holding on to her hips, nails digging into her flesh like she's his only lifeline. Kate suddenly stops clawing against the sheets when she sees who's behind Gary.

She sees herself, completely naked and holding the knife she used to cut Gary's meatloaf a couple hours ago. Herself, covered head to toe in slime and blood and the viscera she was born in, sliding right out of Kate herself just before her husband came home. This second Kate has a handful of Gary's hair, is pulling his head back as hard as she can, his neck opening like a Pez dispenser. The look of rage Kate sees on her double's face is astounding. She had no idea she was capable of that look, realizes in that moment, seeing the supernovas of her eyes, exactly where all her pent-up rage and anger went. At Gary. At John. At Trinity Springs and her life here.

Even at herself.

The second Kate gives a single, rough yank and Gary's hands claw off of her, he's rip-corded out of her and totters across the room, knocking over a lamp and flopping violently to the floor, his hands finally around his throat trying to staunch the blood, but it's far too late for that.

Kate turns in place on the bed, pulling the sheets up and around her to cover herself, a force of habit she developed after her marriage had dipped quickly down into its nadir. She pulls her legs up away from the floor like there's a monster under the bed as Gary stares her down from across the room. But it's too late for him to do anything. Not just a few moments too late, but years, decades. It became too late the moment Kate realized it was better to bottle it up than to actually address it, too late the moment Gary began thinking of Kate as a maid he could fuck rather than his wife.

His hands slip away from his throat and he stares up at the ceiling, forever unblinking.

The second Kate, the naked Kate, the also-covered-in-blood Kate, looks at the first.

"What do we do?" she asks. Her voice is identical.

Kate knows.

The river.

part 3
Entrée

COCKTAIL HOUR

The house is just as enormous inside. Far more lavish than Sorrel can ever hope to even imagine affording on her waitressing tips. Ludicrous in its ostentatiousness. It reminds her of a museum; statues in an ancient Greek style flank the entrance, which is all she really needs to know about the level of money in this place. Even so, she still sees the chandelier dangling above their heads, the central staircase before them leading up to the second-floor balcony, the tile floor polished to a reflective sheen. It's the kind of house that has *wings*. Sorrel can't begin to imagine how far back it goes or what kind of setup is in the backyard.

She refuses to call this place *Maud's house*.

"John, honey, why don't you take her into the sitting room? I'll check on dinner."

"Sure thing." John looks at Sorrel and gestures towards a room—it's so far away she's worried they'll have to jog to get to it—as Maud vanishes into what Sorrel guesses in the kitchen. John walks ahead of Sorrel and does not touch her. It seems a very deliberate, conscious decision on his part. Something he wants her to notice him not doing. But what she does notice is his eyes, the way he narrows them at her in a way that says, *I could if I wanted to, and there would be nothing you could do to stop me.*

In a way, it's the ultimate show of control, of power. Of force.

Sorrel follows him into the sitting room. It's a small library, with built-in shelves and big, comfortable-looking lounge chairs with cupholders in the armrests. Sorrel tries to scan the spines of the books, hopes they'll give her some kind of clue. All she can see is they're old and leatherbound, titles long since worn away, before Maud arrives, a drink in each hand. She hands John what looks like an old fashioned, some kind of brandy with a cherry in it. Sorrel gets what smells like straight whiskey with a single, large square of ice. The smell of the alcohol takes her back to last night, threatens something sick at the back of her throat, but she holds it down.

That was too fast. What, ten seconds? The drinks must have been waiting. But waiting how? *How* to this entire thing? How to the invitation, to the strange room with the switchboard woman. This whole neighborhood and its people.

"Enjoy," Maud says, and when Sorrel looks at her, she realizes the how doesn't matter. She doesn't care about the how. All she cares about is Maud.

With the drink in her hand, Sorrel's training kicks in; she didn't see this drink get made. She cannot consume it.

But Maud made it. Didn't she?

Sorrel doesn't sip from it. Maud doesn't seem to notice. She merely bends over slightly, her hands on her knees—Sorrel trying to avoid looking down her blouse, an old habit, despite the situation—and smiles that same frigid smile.

"Why don't you two get to know one another? I'm going to go into the kitchen and help the cook with dinner."

A cook, Sorrel thinks, now doubly suspicious of the drink. She wasn't sure she can trust it because she wasn't sure she can trust Maud. But now she knows with certainty she can't trust it. Who knows who's on the other side of that kitchen door? She listens, and can hear nothing but shuffling, the occasional clatter of plates, the hiss of something on the stovetop. So they're not alone in the house. But who knows where this cook's loyalties lie?

John is across the room, sliding a record out of its sleeve and putting it down onto the turntable. And when he does, Maud whispers something lower, something only Sorrel can hear.

It's everything Sorrel can do to hold on to her cocktail, to not let it drop and shatter, its brown guts spill across the floor. So instead she holds onto it tight, too tight, suddenly afraid it'll shatter in her hand. She sits down before her legs buckle under her, replaying the secret message Maud has passed to her, their translated idioglossia echoing in Sorrel's head.

Don't eat anything.

PERSEPHONE

Sorrel sits with a drink in her hand she has absolutely no intention of drinking. John, on the other hand, takes a long, slow sip of his, and Sorrel knows the action is meant to taunt her. *Go ahead*, that sip says. *Drink yours*. He knows she won't. And she knows she won't.

But by god does she want to. Needs something to mellow her out. Especially after what Maud just whispered to her: *Don't eat anything*. Sorrel was already leaning towards that. She didn't see this drink get made. There was no way she was taking it. When she thought of whatever food awaited in the kitchen, all she could think about was the old myth of Persephone and the pomegranate seed. She ate food from the Underworld, and then she had to stay there.

But Maud knew their idioglossia. She remembered. And she'd spoken it like it was her first language, not something they'd made up and struggled with and laughed about. She was fluent, urgent.

That meant she was really in there. All Sorrel had to do was get her alone, and because of something John said earlier, she knew exactly when that moment would come. All she had to do was stall.

"So," Sorrel says, hoping her voice doesn't crack, "how did you and Maud meet?"

"Ah, it's a lovely story." John shifts in his seat. Sorrel can already tell he's the kind of man who likes to talk about himself. Those kind are always easy to spot. So let him talk. Let him go on for as long as he wants. It'll just be less time Sorrel herself has to kill. There's a moment coming, she knows. John spilled it earlier. He thinks he's slick, but he messed up, and Sorrel knows her chance for escape is close at hand. She can bide her time for the length of a simple, polite conversation. Especially if he's filling in most of it. Like men tend to do.

"It was in church. I was outside the neighborhood, checking up on a few potential tenants. I go every Sunday, we have a fine church here, but I think it's healthy to see how the other half lives from time to time, you know? To remind us to be grateful for everything we have. So, I was there, and I laid my eyes on the most wondrous little creature." He looks towards the kitchen as if he can see Maud. And maybe he can. What did Sorrel know? The rules of this place are clearly different. Maybe the rules of John are different too. "I went back the following week and saw her again, and I knew it was special because I had no other reason to be outside. Me being me, rather shy, I couldn't even *dream* of gathering the courage to speak to such a heavenly beauty on that first day." Sorrel grimaces despite herself as he continues, "But the second time, when I saw her again, I knew it was something that was meant to be. It was a sign, that she was the one for me." Of course this man would think that, that a woman was a thing created to please him. "I talked her parents into allowing me to court her."

Now, that's something Sorrel gave more credence to. This man, with his rakish eyes, his Cary Grant smile. Such an image, the idea of courtship itself, would have greatly appeased Maud's "family values" parents. So much so that they may have even been willing to overlook whatever deviance he has lurking underneath.

John smiles, takes a sip of his drink. "The rest, as they say, is history."

"That *is* a lovely story," Sorrel lies with a fake, pretentious smile. *It's also a bullshit story.* The Maud who Sorrel remembers was spiritual, but not religious. Her overzealous parents had unintentionally gifted her with a disdain for organized religion. She was never one of the anti-God kids they knew in school, the kind who said nothing mattered because it was cool and edgy. She once told Sorrel she didn't believe everything happened for a reason, but that they were the reason everything happened.

But then the thought of change crept into Sorrel's head again; how much could people change over almost a decade? Could Maud have found God somewhere in that time? Maybe, if her mother had anything to say about it.

Sorrel hears a clacking of heels against tile, and turns around as Maud comes back into the room.

"Dinner's almost ready, honey," Maud says to John.

Sorrel catches a glance over Maud's shoulder, sees the kitchen door swing shut, and just for a moment spies another face. It's a young woman, light-skinned but still Black, plating something on the kitchen island. She spies Sorrel just as Sorrel looks at her, but then the door closes, cutting them off from one another, too quick for Sorrel to see any real expression.

Who are you? Sorrel wonders, a flurry of emotions flitting through her. A stranger meant the woman could be dangerous. But she is a woman. She is Black. Two points in the column closer to Sorrel. But being closer, being similar to her, doesn't necessarily mean friendly, she knows. People could self-sabotage. People could self-hate. People could think they were so unlike other people who were just like them, people they thought were beneath them.

Sorrel is pulled back to herself when Maud touches her arm.

"Why don't you come and take a look at some of my clothes. I'm sure I have something that fits you that you could wear for dinner."

This is it. This is the moment Sorrel's been waiting for. The moment she'll be alone with Maud, John and his polite demeanor trapped downstairs while the women go upstairs to change. She chances a glance at him and his stupid, smiling face, and it's still stupid, and smiling. He tips his drink to Sorrel ever so slightly, like he knows exactly what she's up to, *Go ahead. Try it. It won't make a difference.*

Sorrel leaves her untouched drink and follows Maud up the stairs near the entrance of the house. Her hammering heart feels like it's going to blow out her ribcage.

This is how I felt whenever I would look at you, she thinks, watching Maud go up the stairs in front of her. *I felt like I was going to die. But also like I'd never been more alive.*

Sorrel is vaguely aware of the geography of the second floor of the house, but such a triviality has taken a backseat to her new opportunity. She knows there are wings of the house, but follows Maud in a beeline to the master bedroom. It is just as opulent as everywhere else. As big as the sitting room. A massive four poster bed, curtains dangling from the canopy. There's dressers on either side, and a vanity to the left. Sorrel imagines Maud sitting in front of it, those naked lightbulbs illuminating her face. Towards the back of the bedroom, Sorrel can see deep into a walk-in closet on one side, and the immaculate corner of a bright-tiled bathroom on the other.

"It's nice, isn't it?" Maud shuts the door behind them.

I remember the first time this happened. I remember you shutting the door behind me in your ratty, cluttered childhood bedroom. We told your mother we were going to listen to CDs. At least that was our actual intention. We didn't do it for very long. You had a poster for the rock band Darrow Foroi on your wall, and I stared up at it while you kissed your way down my belly. Sorrel remembers the exact same thing happening that day, remembers turning, seeing

Maud leaning back against the door, a devilish look on her face. She remembers thinking, *What are you going to do to me?* in a way that was scary but excited, like being in line for a roller coaster.

"We're alone now," Maud says, "just us gals." But she doesn't suddenly drop the act. Sorrel sees the ghost of that old devilish smile on her face, and then confusion.

"What?" Sorrel asks, stuped, kicking herself for not saying more.

"Nothing," Maud waves a hand in front of her face. "I just got the strangest feeling of déjà vu. It's not important. Wait until you see what I've got for you." Maud passes in front of her, heading into the walk-in closet, and Sorrel is so stupidly frozen with shock and indecision that she can't even reach out and grab Maud's arm, despite how much she's willing her body to do it.

Inside the closet, Maud flicks a light switch and illuminates what looks more like a small bedroom. Sorrel follows Maud to the threshold, pulled by the invisible tether that connects them. She watches Maud sort through all her dresses, looking for the right one. Judging by the closet, it doesn't look like Maud owns a pair of pants at all. Pantsuits are probably not allowed in this place. They'd probably burn up in the atmosphere.

"You're lucky we're so nearly the same size," Maud says, looking for the right color. "I don't know why you always wanted to wear such frumpy clothes. You always looked so nice dressed up." Her eyes lift from the dresses for a moment, and her brows furrow in that confused look again. "I remember that," she mutters to herself. "How do I remember? *What* do I remember?"

Somehow, even though Sorrel knew this was coming, she's completely unprepared for the moment they're finally alone. *What do I do? What do I say? Why hasn't Maud dropped this act? She clearly remembers* something. She feels helpless. In a bad way. Like she can do nothing except stand there and wait for this horror to continue. Not like the way Maud used to make her feel. Like she could do nothing except stand there and wait for Maud to come to her.

How does this work? What do I do? How do I tell you what I feel? Sorrel finds herself unable to direct the conversation, merely follow along in Maud's wake. "I like my frumpy clothes. You used to, too," she says, long ago learning why exactly that was—the bigger, the baggier, the more easily they hid her and the body that was so far from the standard of beauty. The better she could navigate the world and pretend to be something else. Anything else other than what she was and how she was trapped.

But she never felt trapped with Maud. Whenever they were together she felt released, free. Maud had always known, always been able to see what Sorrel really wanted, and help guide her to it.

And then it clicks. She knows exactly what to do. Take the leap.

Sorrel walks all the way into the closet after Maud, walking just the way Maud used to after her. Almost like Sorrel was prey in a little game. And Maud looks the same way Sorrel knows she always used to. Like she can't wait to be eaten. Like such a thing would cause a transformation she could not accomplish on her own. A rebirth. Coming out the other side as something new, something beautiful. The thing she was always meant to be.

Sorrel comes right up to her, and even though Maud's taller than her she grabs her by the wrists. Sorrel can feel Maud struggle in her grasp, just like she used to struggle in Maud's. Pretending like she wanted to get away, secretly wanting to be held tighter, to never be let go, to be held against the dangers of the world.

Pulling her closer, Maud lets out a little gasp that's more excited than frightened.

They are alone, but Sorrel still uses their idioglossia, hoping against hope that Maud will remember, that the words, the sounds, will draw her back to herself. She tells her, *You know what we were.*

She can see it in Maud's eyes, the confused recognition. The knowing something is important a moment before realizing exactly how. She blinks rapidly, looking both at Sorrel and away, like she expects this all to be some kind of joke. But there's recognition in her eyes. Sorrel can see it. She just has to fish it out.

"What we were..." Maud whispers. "We weren't just friends."

"No." Slowly, so as not to break the moment, Sorrel reaches up and holds Maud's face in her hands. Maud is skittish, but she lets her, coming closer once Sorrel's fingertips touch her.

"We weren't just friends."

It's at that moment that it all crashes down. Maud collapses into a wordless sob, throws a hand over her mouth as her legs fail her, as she reaches out for Sorrel, for the dresses hanging from the closet, for anything that will hold her. She catches nothing, but Sorrel catches her. Holds her. Gently guides her down to the floor. She pulls Maud into her arms, and knows for sure, is absolutely certain now, that this is the real Maud.

This is *her* Maud.

They are together again.

JOHN

John knows the ladies are going to be a while. That's alright. He has something to tend to, one last piece of their meal that still needs to be prepped. He swigs the last of his drink and places it in the armrest of the chair. Someone else will get it later. What matters is it won't be him. That's the whole point of this place. So he, the man of the house, won't have to. John gets up and strides across the room, into the kitchen.

The cook is standing there, the dark girl—or are you supposed to say African-American now?—eyes downcast at the floor. Her time is coming to an end, John can feel. After all, she's getting old. Unsatisfying to look at. He's had the same one for so long. Years, in fact. Even longer than he's been married to Maud. Yes, it's certainly time to trade up to this year's model. He thinks about it and knows he's right. Sorrel will do just fine. She's young, fresh, strong of body and weak of mind, like the rest of their kind. It wasn't cruel, it was only natural. Everyone has their place, and John knows where hers is, even if she doesn't. She'll be perfect.

"It's time to get the main course ready," John says.

The cook says, "Yes, sir," and turns around to take a ring of keys off the wall. John doesn't notice the way her throat bobs, like she's trying to hold back something disgusting.

"Wait for me here," John says.

Again, the cook says nothing other than, "Yes, sir," keeping her eyes down to the floor and away from him.

Not once does it ever—has it ever—crossed John's mind to think of this woman as a person, a human being. Not any of them. Not a single one. To him, his cook and everyone else tending to Trinity Springs are worth no more than the servant characters in his favorite pictures. Less, actually. At least the ones in films are entertaining. They sing, they dance, they play the piano. The ones here at Trinity Springs are just train conductors and waiters and bartenders milling about in the background. People who are there to exist only as vehicles for the pleasures of the real characters, whether they're simple ones like making John's dinner or his drinks, or darker, more heinous desires. Not once has it really occurred to him to think his cook might have a past, that she might have had a family at one point, that there could be people somewhere missing her. And if any of those thoughts do occur, they're fleeting bugs, there only for a moment before they even have time to register, and then they're lost in the blinding white brightness of his own supposed superiority.

Instead of thinking these things, in fact, forgetting about the presence of the cook entirely, John pokes his head out of the kitchen and looks up the staircase.

Listening.

His hearing is better than most, especially in this place, in *his* place, and he can hear, from the master bedroom, the soft sounds of sobbing. Muffled, like someone is attempting to hide it from him.

He smiles.

His mouth too big. His teeth too many.

Those sounds are delicious, even if they mean that perhaps Maud has woken up. That that awful woman, Sorrel, has found some way of reaching the woman his wife used to be. And after everything he's done to make sure she stays loyal. Obedient. *His.* All the times he's fed her, like even yesterday, making sure she had her sandwich as soon as they got home. Making sure she was fit enough to provide the meal for tonight's supper even. After all he's done for her, she's reverting back to her old self.

Even if that's the case, if she is back to the woman she used to be, it doesn't matter. There's nothing they can do now. Not now they're in his world. It'll only be a matter of time until she's back to being his dutiful wife.

John walks away from the stairs and back into the kitchen, the cook waiting right where he left her. On his gesture she walks over to what at first appears to be a pantry door in the kitchen. She searches for the key ring, finds the right one. Unlocks it. Opens it. Steps aside for John.

Instead of a pantry, there is a set of deepening stairs, stairs that look like they're carved directly into the earth beneath the house. Stairs that lead to a basement with no light.

Dinner's almost ready.

He can almost smell it.

DRESSED TO KILL

Sorrel pulls Maud away from her just long enough to talk. She doesn't want to, fights every instinct in her body that tells her to keep the two of them held together. Like maybe if she tries hard enough she can squeeze so tight they'll become one being, and it's there that they'll be safe.

"Maud." Sorrel stares into her eyes. It takes her another moment to come to, another moment to remember where she is and who she's with. It isn't until she sees lucidity in her eyes that Sorrel tells her, "We're getting out of here, okay? I need you to tell me how we get out of this town." She can see it in her eyes; she doesn't know. She barely knows where they are right now.

"Alright," Sorrel says, more to herself than Maud. "We're going to get out of here. And he's not going to follow us. Okay?"

Maud nods, but Sorrel doesn't think she's really heard her.

Sorrel thinks about how she got into Trinity Springs, about where she should be in the geography of the world she was familiar with. It doesn't make any sense. She went through the house and the waiting room, and yet she'd also seen the car at both the diner and Trinity Springs. Was that it? Was the car their way out? John certainly couldn't have taken it through the waiting room. It was as good a theory as any. And even if it didn't work out, it would mean they would have a car and John would not. Sorrel could at the very least put real ground, real miles, between them and him.

Assuming any of this was real ground.

"Come on," she says, hauling Maud to her feet. "We're getting out of here."

But when they turn around he's there. In the threshold of the walk-in closet, leaning up against the jam. He's not making it look like he's blocking the doorway, but he is. They all know it.

"Ladies, what is taking so long?" he says it charmingly, like he's really everything he pretends to be. Sorrel sees something, or maybe thinks she sees something; one of his eyes bulging momentarily, one larger than the other. But it's there and gone before she can really understand what she saw.

John looks over Sorrel's shoulder at Maud. "Honey?"

She says nothing. Cowers.

"I think," John says, taking a step into the closet, "our guest would look lovely in this one." He picks a simple, black dress off the rack. Holds it out to Sorrel.

It hangs there between them for the longest time. Like a challenge. A dare. *Go ahead. Smack it out of my hand.* Sorrel wants to think she can, wants to think she could take him. There has to be some sharp object, some weapon she could use to harm him. She knows she could.

She hopes she could.

But she doesn't think she should take the chance. Not here, not now. Not with him blocking the only way out. She has to be smart about this. She has to play each card perfectly.

So she takes the dress.

"Excellent," John says. "I'll be downstairs. Dinner's almost ready."

THE DINNER BELL

"You have to do it", Maud said to her. "You have no idea what he'll do if we disobey". But she has some idea. Sadistic men aren't as imaginative as they believe themselves to be. "Just put on the dress," Maud begged her, before hurrying out of the closet and into the bathroom to fix her makeup.

Sorrel stands in the closet alone now, the door shut, pulling the dress over her head. She does that before she takes the rest of her clothes off, absolutely refusing to be naked in this new and hostile environment. The dress, of course, has no goddamn pockets, holds tight against her skin. She has no idea how she can conceal a weapon of any kind on her person.

Smart fucker, Sorrel thinks, remembering to not knock John down too many pegs. Don't underestimate him. Of course that's the point, the reason he picked this one for her. Sorrel looks at herself in the closet's floor-length mirror once she's wearing the dress and nothing else. It clings to her in a way nothing off the rack ever has, a way that makes her think it was tailored for her. Does the strangeness of this place have something to do with it? Is this place making sure there isn't a single lump or fold that doesn't hug her body, something that makes her presentable for him? Does it somehow turn this dress into a garb that is made not for her, but for others' enjoyment of her? To show her off. To objectify her. After all, it's Maud's.

Sorrel takes the heels that Maud left her, for a moment looks longingly at her sneakers that stand next to her piled-up clothes. She'd prefer to keep those nearby, knows she'll need them for running, but she can just as easily go barefoot. She won't love it, but it'll be more practical than snapping the heels off her shoes and trying to run, an impossibility Sorrel awkwardly giggles at.

You're laughing, she thinks to herself. *Don't know if that's good or proof you've already lost it.* It would've been easy, under these circumstances.

Sorrel leaves the closet and walks back out into the bedroom. She can hear the faucet in the bathroom running, and while Maud fixes her makeup, Sorrel quickly shuffles over to the window.

Locked. From the outside.

"That won't work."

Sorrel jumps and turns around, sees Maud in the doorway to the bathroom. Her makeup is back to normal. Well, normal for wherever here is. Sorrel can see it in her eyes, knows this is the real Maud, this is *her* Maud, here to stay. "That won't work," she says again. "He wants there to only be one way in or one way out." When she speaks, she doesn't use their idioglossia, doesn't talk like they're being watched. So, no cameras or microphones. At least, that she's aware of. That wouldn't fit the aesthetic of this place, Sorrel thinks. So, more like no husbands leering just outside the door.

"Maud," Sorrel says, coming over to her, taking her by the shoulders. "Who is this guy? How did you get here? How do we get out?"

But Maud isn't listening to her. She's trying not to cry again.

"Dinner is almost ready. The cook's downstairs working on it. But, listen to me, you can't eat here, not *anything* from here." Suddenly she grabs Sorrel's shoulders right back, her eyes clear like she's finally lucid. "You haven't eaten anything from here, have you?"

"No. I didn't even drink the drink."

Maud smiles ever so slightly. "Good. Good, that's good."

"What happens if I eat?" Sorrel asks, and then thinks that maybe she'd rather not know. For a brief moment she imagines herself dolled up like Maud. She's about to glide past it, tell Maud to forget about it, but she gets an answer.

"The food, it does something to you. But especially the meat. If you eat, you'll stay."

Jesus, maybe this *is* Hell.

"Is that what happened to you?" Sorrel asks. "Did you eat something from here?"

There's something in Maud's eyes, something so close to the surface, but it can't bring itself to breach.

"Okay, forget about that for now. Maud, do you know how to get out of this place?" Their options are limited. They're running out of time. Sorrel doesn't really know what they can do besides steal the car and drive. She has a horrible invasive thought, an image that plows itself into her head. Sorrel and Maud driving the car, and then an invisible camera pans up and up and up and Trinity Springs just keeps going forever and ever. An entire planet made up of identical houses and manicured lawns and smiling, happy people.

No, no, that's not possible. But what does she know? Where they're standing shouldn't be possible. But they have to try. They have to do something.

Maud thinks about it, the look on her face displaying the struggle of her attempt at recollection.

"I was always with John when I went outside. Which was usually so he could interview people about getting houses here. He always said the border was dangerous."

Sorrel hates the familiarity of that.

"What border, hun?"

"There's a border to this place. It's how he keeps people out. And in."

A border. Sorrel imagines an enormous wall surrounding the place. It is a gated community after all. They needed to get to it first.

"Maud, where does John keep his car keys?"

Maud's fingers suddenly grip her tight, digging into her arms.

"Wait, no, we can't go outside after sundown." And then she suddenly, horrifyingly corrects herself. "*You* can't go outside after sundown."

And there it is again, John's subtle threat laid bare, the horrible honesty brought to the surface.

Trinity Springs is a sundown town.

That's when a bell, an actual dinner bell, rings.

DINNER IS SERVED

Sorrel can smell the meal from the top of the stairs. It's unlike anything she's ever smelled before. A scent she can't place. It smells saucy, buttery, but with some burned edge she can't identify.

"What is that?" she whispers to Maud.

"It doesn't matter," Maud says, but the look in her eyes tells Sorrel it very much does. It tells her it's something horrible. "Don't eat it." She hurries down the stairs, tries to pull Sorrel with her, but Sorrel stops. "What are we doing? We have to get out of here."

Maud says, "He'll catch us if we leave now. Just get him talking. Stall."

"And then what? What's the plan?"

"I—I don't know. Come on—he won't like it if we're late." She pulls Sorrel after her, leads her down the stairs, through the kitchen and to the dining room.

There hasn't been enough time to get a spread this big set up. How long was she upstairs with Maud? Twenty minutes? Max? Something like this, it would've taken hours. And with far more than two people. But then Sorrel remembers the mysterious cook she glimpsed for a moment. There must be more people around the house somewhere. After all, it had to take more than one to set all this up; the long dining table is covered with an elegant, white tablecloth and completely filled with food. And there's John sitting at the head.

"Ah, there are my gals." He rises as they approach, gestures for Maud to sit at his right, Sorrel his left. Sorrel looks at what's laid out. Half of the food she can't even identify, it's so fancy. Vegetables are easily recognizable. Crackers and unknown soups. But there's also a big hunk of meat that Sorrel first takes to be a ham. But the meat is far too dark. Covered in some kind of sauce. The meat is what that strange barbecue smell is coming from. This close, the sickly-sweet smell makes Sorrel gag a little.

It reminds her of roadkill.

Sorrel refuses to let her eyes linger on the meat tenderizer, two-pronged fork, the carving knife. She clocks them, but she can't let John see her eyes linger on them, or the fire in her eyes when she imagines what she can do with them.

"I had a fresh drink made for you," John says, pointing to it. "Yours was starting to get watered down." Of course he knows she didn't touch it. Why did all the worst ones have to be so goddamn observant?

Sorrel sits as Maud does, the layout of their escape already in her mind. The front door is right behind her. Just through a doorway into the foyer. She could make it out easily. Maybe hit John with something long enough to stun him. But Maud is on the whole other side of the table. She would have to get around him or go over the table itself in order to make it to the front door. Smart man. He knows exactly what he's doing in keeping her here. And that's to say nothing of the other people in the house. How many of them are there? Whose side are they on? If a fight broke out, would they intervene?

Sorrel thinks maybe they can get John drunk, get him sloppy, maybe that'll give them an advantage. But he's a big man. How much booze can he handle? Could Sorrel drag that out before the smell of the meat made her sick? Could they drag that on long enough before he realizes they aren't eating anything?

Sorrel looks across the table at Maud, who gives her just the slightest, almost imperceptible shake of her head. Maud is very nearly crying.

"So, Sorrel," John turns to her, stuffing a napkin into his shirt collar. "Tell me about yourself. Do you have a man in your life?"

A man. No. Absolutely not. She briefly thinks about the guy from the bar last night, but she can't even remember his name. Barely even remembers what they did together. Nevertheless, she invokes a self-defense technique every woman learns. *My brother and his friends are waiting outside.*

"Yeah." She nods. "Pete," she says, not knowing if that was actually the guy's name or just the first name that pops into her head.

And then an idea hits her. Talking. Yes, if she was talking, she wasn't eating. Maybe that can buy her enough time to figure out what to do next. Plus, she's now certain that if she puts any of that meat into her mouth, she's going to throw it up.

"Ah, and what does Pete do?" The way he says Pete, it's with emphasis, like inverted commas around the name. He's not buying it, not yet.

She remembers a man wolf-whistling at her on the street. "He's a construction worker. Foreman, actually." She looks over at Maud, not knowing how, but silently willing her thoughts across the table. *Don't worry, there's no Pete. There's just you. Only you.* She feels compelled to reassure her, despite the fact they're sitting there with Maud's supposed husband.

"Ah, good, good. Nice strong job for who sounds like a nice strong fella. Hate to see so many men these days taking all these *barista* or *secretary* jobs." He says the words with such obvious disdain. Across the table, Maud winces.

Service jobs, you mean, Sorrel thinks. *God forbid you take a job where you have to do something for somebody else. A job that you think should be for a* woman. And, hell, maybe she doesn't have to talk the entire time. Maybe, like she suspected before, she just has to let John fill it until she can come up with something better than *bolt out the front door.*

"What about you?" she asks. "What do you do?"

"Oh," John cuts off a piece of the strange meat and pops it in his mouth. "A little of this, a little of that. Fingers in a lot of pies, as they say." The sight of him chewing it makes her nauseous, even though he does it with politeness, dabbing at his mouth with his napkin. "You know they always tell you to have multiple revenue streams. The biggest is that my father was one of the founders of Trautman Oil, oh, when was that, thirty...four? Before the war. It's been a long time." He smiled.

Before the... *World War II?*

Sorrel looks over to Maud as if to confirm if she's hearing this correctly. Maud has a couple pieces of that meat on her plate, but she isn't eating, just watching John attentively. Like a good wife. But Sorrel can see behind her eyes, knows she's working to figure out something, anything.

"We're in a lot of American companies," he says, clearly on a tangent now. "I'm on the board for MacReady's Superstore, I work with Darrow Pharmaceutical. But my biggest thing, my passion, is food. I've always been a chef."

"So, why didn't you make dinner?"

"I have people for that now," he smiles. "I get the same result without any of the effort. It really is the way of the future. I—Sorrel, you're not eating. You really should try it," John says, motioning towards the hunk of meat. "It's delicious." But he doesn't wait for her to respond at all before he keeps dominating the conversation. "You'll have to tell me the name of the company Pete works for. Maybe we'll hire them when we want to expand. Construction, it's a good pursuit," he says, "Noble. A continuation of Manifest Destiny in my opinion. But here in Trinity Springs, those are the kinds of jobs we save for, well, the people with the certain physical aptitudes for it." He looks at Sorrel, winks.

Sorrel knows exactly the kinds of people he means. She remembers seeing them on the way in. Now that she feels like her brain might actually have the space for it, she wonders what their stories are. How did the people she saw trimming gardens and picking up trash cans end up here? She doubts very much it was willingly. And if it wasn't, can she leave them here while she took Maud? Is she capable of something like that?

"So, tell me," John says, "why isn't this Pete with us tonight?"

Sorrel shrugs. "Busy, I guess. He's got a lot of important stuff to handle. He doesn't concern me with all the details, you know how it is." Appeal to his ego, stroke his misogyny. Yes, she's involved with a very busy, very important man. She doubts John Kelly possesses any fear of someone like the theoretical Pete—or, hell, maybe any human being at all—but maybe that would get him relaxed at the very least. She needs more time. That smell is clogging her mind.

"Building things," John says, more to himself than either of the women. "Yes, yes, very important to keep America going strong." He takes a sip of his drink. "I'm assuming his crew is all migrants?"

Sorrel plays dumb again. "I wouldn't know." The majority of John's crew certainly appears to be. *Migrants*, sure, a gross over-simplification. Kidnap victims more like. She didn't see a single pale face out there that afternoon. If there are any in the house now, she suspects the same thing.

"So, what's preoccupying him tonight?"

Sorrel knows what he's after, knows he's trying to get her to slip up. She finds it harder and harder to think the longer she's forced to smell that hunk of meat. She blinks slowly-forming tears out of her eyes, tries to subtly shake her head. There's too much going on. She can't sit here and smell that and try to think of an escape and deal with the possibility that the other people she saw are captives too and maybe the fact that there are more of them in the house and who knows where their loyalties lie and try to keep up a normal conversation she's gonna crack under all the pressure.

"Honey," Maud says, gesturing to John's slowly-emptying cup, "would you like another drink?"

Sorrel knows she's filling in the blank spaces for her, trying to keep his attention.

John looks at his cup, then up at Maud.

"They'll get it when I'm ready," he says, brushing her off, and gesturing to a small bell Sorrel only just now notices.

You've got to be fucking joking.

"So," John says, returning his attention to Sorrel, "is Pete work-ing now?"

"I wouldn't think so," she says. "It is dark out. Though, I don't really understand his job. I kinda just see to stuff around the house." She tells him what she knows he wants to hear. Poor little housefrau, too silly and fanciful to understand the intricacies of her big, strong man's work.

John just nods as if he's agreeing with her thoughts. "Quite right, quite right."

Christ, is this guy going to whip out a fucking phrenology textbook next?

"So, how did you come across such a nice home?" Sorrel asks.

"Ah," John exhales as if he's been waiting for this question all night. He leans back in his chair. "It's actually a family home."

Of-fucking-course it is.

"I stay at home," Maud says like she's proud of it. There's nothing wrong with that on the face of it, it just seems so strange coming out of Maud's mouth. The old Maud... That was never something she wanted. She'd referred to it as a cage. She had no idea how right she'd eventually become.

"You stay here, even with the help?" Sorrel asks.

Maud nods. "There's a lot to do in a place this big." She pauses for a moment, eyeing John subtly, and then adds, "It's a privilege to maintain the home for my husband. Especially in such a unique place."

"Plus," John says, "someone needs to keep an eye on *them*." The help, he means.

Sorrel sees Maud's disgusted look. Thankfully, John doesn't. He empties his drink and reaches for the bell, rings it. It tinkles a small, tinny sound that echoes throughout the house in a strange way Sorrel isn't expecting. It's like how something sounds in a room without furniture.

A moment later, the door to the kitchen opens, and a young, light-skinned Black woman walks in, her eyes cast downward. She hides it after the first step or two, but Sorrel sees it; the woman's walking with a slight limp. She has a black long-sleeved blouse, black pencil skirt, dark stockings, and black heels. So little of her skin is shown, and combined with the limp, Sorrel has a dark, terrible thought of what has happened to her in this house. The woman places a refill of John's drink on the table before him.

He doesn't acknowledge her presence. Doesn't even say thank you. He takes the glass without giving her a second glance. Except when she turns toward the rest of the table, when John's eyes lecherously take in her backside.

Maud says, "Thank you, that'll be all," perhaps quicker than she should have, clearly attempting to get the woman out of there.

She nods and noiselessly vanishes back into the kitchen.

Sorrel looks across the table at Maud, but her expression is unreadable.

John asks, "Has Maud told you the history of the place?" His return to normal conversation is startling. A loud clap that pulls

Sorrel off of her own mental rails. She can't just go back to their old conversation after what she's just witnessed.

"Who..."

"Don't worry about her," John says, waving the thought away. "Just one of the help." The way he says it is like he's stretching, like he can't actually remember who she is or what she does. Like she's that unimportant.

John plows ahead. "My great-grandfather found this place, you know. Or perhaps great-great? I'm not so sure, I'd have to check the records. Anyway, like any new place, it belonged to someone else before the Kelly family."

So they took it. Did it belong to the ancestors of people like their maid? The workers Sorrel saw outside?

"An American tradition." Sorrel is deadpan, her eyes locking with John's.

He stares right back at her and beams. "The way the story was always told to me, is that the very first time any Kelly ever came here, this place was empty. Total nothingness. Just an endless expanse. A void. Except for a man. Just one man. The previous owner. Or, so he appeared to be, anyway. A man sitting here in the middle of all this nothing. All this space, all this potential, and here he was sitting in the middle of an empty void. Once this place belonged to us, we built all this." John waves his hands around, indicating not just the room, not just the house, Sorrel knows, but the whole of Trinity Springs. "Story of America, you know? Manifest Destiny."

"And how much did they pay this lone man for his land?" Sorrel asks, eyes like daggers. She doesn't care about any of John's story time bullshit, she's heard it all before in one way or another. She tries not to glance toward the kitchen, the woman. She looks at John, but doesn't really pay attention to him. And that smell is still working its way through her, making her head heavy. Foggy.

"Manifest Destiny," John said with a smile. "As you may have guessed, we weren't the only ones who eventually came upon this place. There were people like you, of course, who stumbled in by accident, before we really learned how to secure our borders, to build the wall. Some who came on purpose, tried to settle like we did. Many of them we let stay. If they pass our screening process, that is. They make up the families you saw on the way in. And, of course, I go out into the rest of the world recruiting from time to time. But these others... They aren't quite as, shall we say, family values-oriented as we want Trinity Springs residents to be. So, we eventually decided to seal the place off altogether. Built the river, solidified our borders. But every once in a while," he waggles a finger, "there are people who sneak in. Or people we bring in. And those people, well, we have places for them."

The servants, Sorrel thinks. *They really are slaves.*

"And we have a place," John says, "for you."

That's the moment Sorrel knows she's had enough. She can't take the smell of the dinner table anymore, is driven away by all of it; the smell, the man, the very thought of the place she now sits, this horrid microcosm of her country. This terrible compound fracture of a place, infected bone sticking up out of the flesh for her to look at. A core that's ugly and raw. Sorrel shoots up out of her chair so fast she knocks it over. She doesn't even have time to say "*Excuse me*" as she tears off for the bathroom, slamming the door behind her, not enough time to make it to the toilet, or even to the sink, all the way across this stupid-huge bathroom, and so instead she trips into the bathtub and vomits violently yet again.

EXQUISITE

Maud and John listen to Sorrel in the bathroom. The way John tilts his head back, his ear toward the sounds of struggling, it's like he's listening to opera music. Something greatly pleasing to his ears.

It makes her sick. She wonders how she could have ever fallen for such a man, and then doubts she actually had. She knows those feelings can't have been true, that the affection she felt for him can't have been real. She doesn't believe in magic, at least in the way she's always imagined it, but even so thinks John, the existence of Trinity Springs itself, has to be some sort of spell.

Now that she's awake again, that Sorrel has brought the real Maud back to the surface, she realizes there's nothing about John that she has ever found attractive. Certainly he reeks of a man she's been *told* she should feel something for, but her tastes have never leaned classical when it came to any gender. The dark suit. The Cary Grant charm. The polite smiles. He's a man who calls dating courtship, who holds doors, who drapes jackets over puddles in a sidewalk. Maud finds that all so...

Boring.

No, Maud's romantic interests had never been so traditional. She always liked girls more than guys, and mostly liked girls who didn't yet realize they liked girls. She liked to be the assertive one in the relationship, which society typically didn't like and the men themselves liked even less (at least men her own age). Maud liked to guide her partners, to tell them exactly what she wanted, and to coax out of them what they wanted. She found all that with Sorrel, helped her come out of her shell and realize who she really was. Maud felt at peace with her.

None of that is what she feels when she's with John.

What she felt for him was so out of proportion, even compared to the people she normally found herself attracted to. She literally swooned for him. She let him sweep her off her feet so he could carry her away to this place. It was like an intoxicant. No, not *like*. It literally was.

The food.

The first time he'd ever met her, he'd given her a stick of gum. Was that all it took? Maybe all it took to start.

You motherfucker, Maud thinks, looking at his exposed Adam's apple as he leans his head back, listening to the sweet music of Sorrel's vomit spewing forth. *I'm going to kill you*. The knife is so close. So many of them, in fact. It would be so easy to cut his throat right there. Put a fork through his eye. Clobber him with the meat tenderizer. So easy.

Or at least it should be.

But Maud knows the truth. She knows that behind that exterior, there's someone else. She knew it the moment she laid eyes on him in that church basement. It happened like he said, but not *exactly* like he said. AA sure was a place to go if you were looking for desperate, lonely people. And Maud can't think of a time she'd been more desperate and lonely, of another time she would've accepted any offered hand if it meant pulling her out of the hole she'd dug herself into after her family had pulled her away not just from Sorrel, but from everyone else she'd been getting to know. The hole she'd dug herself into after they made her seek priests and therapists, and threatened to send her away somewhere far worse if she didn't straighten out.

That of course eventually led to moving out, to drinking and drugs or binge eating or purging or cutting and wild nights of fucking or anything else that would help take the pain away even for a little bit.

When Maud finally got herself into AA, she learned they never actually called meetings AA until you were inside the room. They were always advertised as "Friends of Tony" or something like that. Saying exactly what they were wouldn't have helped maintain their anonymity. Maud found herself in one of those meetings after yet another bender. It wasn't her first, but midway through she thought it might've been her last. It seemed old hat at first; a couple days off, spending them bouncing from bar to bar, to strip clubs after the bars closed, not for sex—at least not all the time—but for more alcohol. That time, she thought, she must've been going for some kind of record.

She didn't remember what brought it on, but she knew, after a while, what she was trying to bury. Like Sorrel, it was the thought of childhood, the thought of a simpler time. Sitting under the bleachers after school. Sleepovers. Carefree years before she was moved states and a time zone away. It didn't seem like such an insurmountable obstacle at the time. It certainly wouldn't be now, with the advent of social media and Zoom calls. Maud had tried all those things, but Sorrel's web presence was nonexistent, and she eventually resigned herself to the idea that that part of her life was over.

She guessed some part of her reached out through that alcohol haze, had wanted help. She didn't remember looking through her phone for meetings that were running at that very moment, but she must've. She didn't remember going there, but remembered being there. Like the start of a dream, the transition from one place to another completely gone. Maud found herself in a circle of people, the man she would come to call her husband among them.

She knew they didn't like to encourage any potential romantic attachment between you and your sponsor, which kind of put Maud shit out of luck as a pansexual woman. Either way, she didn't think that would be a problem when John came along, with his old-timey suit and his even old-timier attitude. But she neverthe-less found herself drawn to him, found herself letting him pick her up, and she realizes now that each and every time he saw her, he brought with him some food. A piece of gum here, an apple there. Chocolates. Sweets.

He brought her for visits to his neighborhood, a place called Trinity Springs she'd never heard of, and for some reason she couldn't explain, didn't think she'd be able to find her way to again. It always seemed like she was not paying attention, or too hazy-headed, to be able to retrace the actual route to Bender Circle. A couple of times she tried to search the internet for such a name, but always came up blank. She never thought that too strange; people called things different from their normal names all the time.

What she did find strange was how perfect it all was. It was like something out of a fairytale, a romcom where the third act complication was, predictably, smoothed out by simple human communication.

But the whole time Maud could feel something happening, something she wasn't able to articulate or understand until it was far too late. Until she ate the piece of gum, the apple, the chocolates, the sweets.

The price at which that perfection came, and how she lost herself.

The horrible things she'd done to stay in Trinity Springs. She tried not to remember those red moments, the horrible memories she'd buried under the perfectly-cut lawns and the white-picket fences, under waves from neighbors and the sounds of lawn sprinklers. The memories of looking down at her naked self, confused, not knowing what was going on. Or screaming, reaching for help, begging in those moments where she knew what was going to happen to her. And yet every single time, Maud still pointed the captive bolt pistol, still fired at that regurgitated version of herself, mechanically putting down the parts of herself she excised, the parts Trinity Springs wouldn't allow. She swallowed those parts as she was told, allowing the help to prepare the meal, but knowing exactly what she was eating as she chewed, red meat slipping down her throat. Sometimes she ate it prepared; in sandwiches or sliced like ham, chopped up in salads or sizzled like bacon. And sometimes, in those dark moments where she felt more rage and self-hatred than she ever had in her life, more darkness than she ever knew she was capable of feeling, but that was still not enough to put herself out of her own misery, she'd find, her lips and cheeks and teeth stained with blood. She'd eat herself raw. All those memories of the literal parts of herself she'd consumed, becoming someone entirely different.

Destroying herself, eating herself, to become something he would want.

John had pulled her up out of that hole he'd found her in only to put her atop a pedestal. Too late did she figure out it was one she could not get down from. She'd heard of—hell, she'd even experienced—becoming a little more like your partner when you get together. But Maud was someone completely different now.

She was so far afield of who she really was she maybe even forgot who she used to be.

Until she saw Sorrel in that parking lot.

Something was knocked loose inside her then, the old Maud coming back to life, even though she hadn't even realized she was dead. She knew how far she'd gone, how wrong her life had become, and she had a small, if corrupted, idea of how to fix it.

She needed Sorrel. She needed to bring her to Trinity Springs in the same way John brought Maud. Even if Maud knows what John plans to do with Sorrel.

The same thing he had done to Maud.

It was the only way someone like Sorrel would be allowed in Trinity Springs. Someone with her heritage. Someone with her skin. This dark secret wasn't so hidden, even though it was one of the things no one ever talked about. But that's always the thing with people like that, with towns like that, with secrets like that, isn't it? They always think what they were doing was for the greater good. Just thinking of the children. Just looking out for family values. Just keeping the seedy element out of their neighborhood.

Because there was another neighborhood in Trinity Springs. One not for the husbands and the wives, not for the families this place advertised itself as being for, but for those who would serve them. The men and women Maud sees taking out their trash or fixing their roads, tending to their gardens or making their food.

There's another place on the outskirts for them, while they're left to work in, but never live in, this paradise.

They're not even allowed to be here after sundown.

And Maud had thought of putting Sorrel there.

She didn't mean to, knows that even now. But when she saw Sorrel in the parking lot of that diner, the Maud that was buried deep beneath that pastel exterior knew the only way they could be together again was if she came. If she worked. If she was trapped. So she sent the invitation.

Maud knows she is culpable in this, what's happening now. She knows she'll pay for it, that she'll be responsible for whatever happens next. But whatever does happen, she knows now that she's awake, that she's finally herself again. Whatever happens, at least she'll have a choice in it this time.

John opens his eyes and looks across the table at Maud.

"Please," Maud whispers, can't tell where her voice is on the spectrum between pleading and rage. Whatever she decides on will depend on what move John picks next. She has a feeling she already knows. "Don't make her do this."

"Me?" John asks. "You made her do this the moment you decided to invite her." He picks up the carving knife and leaves the table.

Behind him, unnoticed, Maud picks up the meat tenderizer.

SORREL, AGAIN

Sorrel finally falls away from the tub when it feels like she's tossed up all her internal organs. When it feels like she's got nothing left to give, she flops back against the wall, moving her curls so she can feel the cool tile on the back of her neck. Her head spinning, nerves tightened, everything feeling like it's turned up to eleven. The smell of that meat is going to kill her. She doesn't know how much more of that he has in her.

At the very least, it gave her the small blessing of being able to get away from John and his insane ramblings. His family found this place? And it was some sort of void? He sounded drunk. He sounded like he'd lost his mind.

He sounded terrifyingly plausible.

Everything Sorrel has seen since she'd been here, why not add this to the list? Why not some magical in-between space? Why not some strange being inhabiting it? Why not the Kelly family killing it and taking it over? And why not her and Maud being pulled into this orbit, trapped in this insane backwards-world where she can't even go outside after dark, trapped by the whim of some outdated monster of a man?

There are no answers for Sorrel except for her own labored breathing.

No answers until there is one.

A gasp.

From the bathtub.

Sorrel can't see from where she sits leaned up against the wall, but she can certainly feel. It's that animal instinct, the undeveloped sixth sense that tells her something else is in the room with her. That she's not alone. That whatever it is, it's in the tub. But how can that be? There's nothing but Sorrel's own puke in there.

And yet something moves inside it.

Sorrel hears the telltale squeak of something slick moving against the walls and floor of the tub, something trying to get its balance under it. She can see a small distortion of light inside, the brief shadow of something. She backs up, but there's nowhere else to go. Her only other option is back out into the living room.

A hand reaches up over the edge of the tub.

Sorrel screams. Fuck covering her mouth. Fuck John not hearing. Something's crawling out of the goddamn tub, something that should not be there. Sorrel climbs to her wobbly feet, shoes long-ago gone, scattered against the wall somewhere, and climbs up on top of the spacious counter. It's a move for some attempted safety, but part of her wishes she hadn't.

Because from her perch she can see inside the tub.

Her lake of vomit is still there, still its sick gut-color. But inside it is something that wasn't there before, that could not have been there before.

A baby.

Its right arm is huge, distended, the arm of a toddler that clutches the edge of the tub. The baby is silent, doesn't cry at all.

Even when it begins growing.

The rest of the thing grows to match the distorted hand, and even beyond. Limbs plucking out and shifting of their own accord, all moving at different paces but working to the same end. Sorrel eats her own scream as she watches that baby grow in fast-motion into another, life-sized, naked, vomit-covered version of herself.

DOMESTIC VIOLENCE

They hear Sorrel scream from the bathroom.

"Looks like it's time for dinner," John says, taking the carving knife, letting its edge deliberately scrape against the plate as he pulls it away. He wants Maud to hear it, that ring of metal, for her to know in her bones what's about to happen.

But it's that moment that causes Maud to snap. Like that knife has sliced the final string holding her up, the final string tethering her to Trinity Springs, to John. She's known, ever since she saw Sorrel again, that she was going to leave, no matter what it took, even if what it took was death. But the sound of that knife confirmed what she had to do before she did.

Maud watches John head into the other room, and then it's like her body is finally moving of her own accord. Not like she's been when she's been in Trinity Springs; watching, disconnected. Maud reaches across the table and picks up the meat tenderizer, feels its weight in her hand, looks down at her muscles bunch as her body responds to its gravity. She rises from the table, slips out of her high heels so he won't hear her coming, finally feeling her bare feet on the floor, the rest of her body relaxing as she sheds that part of herself. She follows him into the bathroom, finds him in the threshold, raising the knife.

Maud hauls off and clobbers him in the back of the head with the meat tenderizer.

She hits him at an awkward angle. She can feel the hit connect, feel the weight behind it, but instead of plowing into his skull, the head of the tenderizer skirts away at an angle, taking a hunk of John's scalp with it. The scalp hits the door of the bathroom with a wet *thwap*. John buckles. His knees hit the tile and shatter them. He drops the carving knife, reaching out for a handhold of any kind as he does. Maud doesn't let him get a second wind. She pulls the tenderizer back over her head, like she's chopping wood instead of swinging a baseball bat, and strikes with the tenderizer again, hitting John square in the top of the head.

He falls to a useless heap on the floor, blood spraying from the wound—over the walls, on the floor tiles, on Maud's face.

Finally, Maud can see past him, into the rest of the bathroom. She sees her Sorrel, her baby, cowering on top of the counter, screaming silently and flipping her attention from the carnage in the doorway to what's in the bathtub; yet another Sorrel, this one naked and covered in blood and vomit.

So, it's already happened then.

Of course it's already happened. Maud heard it happen. She allowed it to happen. Even though she'd hoped she could spare Sorrel that experience.

Maud steps into the bathroom, over John who she is sure was down-but-not-dead, and grabs her Sorrel by the elbow.

"*Get up.*" When she says it, her voice is just a little deeper. It's the way it used to be before Trinity Springs, before all this chaos, this horror. Before she changed so much of herself for a man. Sorrel can hear that change too. It doesn't completely cleanse her fear, but Maud can see her come back to herself just a little bit. She lets Maud pull her off the counter and they make for the exit, leaving the doppelgänger in the tub.

Just as there's a strong, cold hand around Maud's ankle.

John trips her, and she and Sorrel go spilling into a tumble on the hall floor together, dragging John out of the bathroom with them. He reaches out with his other hand, grabs Maud by the thigh, and begins to crawl his way up her body. When Maud looks back over her shoulder, she sees his face.

John's face is sloughing off his skull. Like it's a Halloween mask several sizes too large. The skin droops and hangs, lips no longer covering teeth, but dripping down to where his chin should be. His eyeballs are no longer visible behind lids, but poking out like little hills behind his forehead. His ears droop down to his jaw and his nose hangs like a useless, impotent hill.

Maud screams.

And then Sorrel hits him with the tenderizer.

The sound is like a thundercrack. Like a bat-breaker of a home run. When Maud looks up, she can see the muscles in Sorrel's bare arms, see her face pulled back in a scowl of rage as she twirls with the backswing of the tenderizer. She hits John so hard that the head of the tenderizer cracks off completely, spinning away down the hall. And then Sorrel's hands are under Maud's arms. She's pulling her away. Maud is kicking with bare feet at John's face and shoulders and hands to get him away from her even though he's limp. She connects with the loose skin on his forehead, and watches in horror as a shred of it sticks between her toes and rips away, revealing what's underneath.

It looks deeply and completely *wrong*. Maud looks into the hole she ripped in his face and what she sees is nothing. Nothing at all. It's a terrible void, quiet and empty, a black hole that draws in even light. A nothingness beyond comprehension.

But Maud doesn't scream. She can't scream. She needs her energy for running, for survival, and she puts all she can into her legs, into getting up as Sorrel pulls her to her feet, into kicking that loose shred of John's face away from her. Sorrel has the car keys, and before she knows it they're out the door.

They're in the drive.

In the car.

The tires are screaming and they're in the street, and Maud is looking back over the rear of the convertible, pushing her whipping hair out of her face as she sees her faceless abomination of a husband standing in the doorway, caught in the indecision of whether he wants to chase them, or Sorrel's double, who's fleeing the opposite way down the street.

FLEE

Sorrel doesn't ask a ton of questions. She figures Maud doesn't have the answers. Besides, there are only two questions that matter, even as they careen through upper-class suburban streets that all look the same goddamn same so there's no sense of direction. The first: "Are you okay?"

She tries to keep her eyes on the road, glancing over at Maud every couple seconds. She looks like herself. Like Maud. A beaten, horrified Maud, but Maud all the same. Maud finds herself for a moment and looks out of the middle space, actually at Sorrel instead of through her. Sorrel can see past the blood, the sweat, the makeup, to Maud, and she knows everything will be okay.

So long as she gets them out of this place.

Leading to the second question that matters: "How do we get out of here?"

All the streets, all the houses, the lawns, everything looks the same. Sorrel tries to remember the different turns John took to get them to the house, but she was too busy being focused on him to recall. It doesn't help that the whole neighborhood looks like it just uses the same five designs over again. Same mailboxes, same houses, same doors, same streets. Like repeating videogame assets. Does she even see the patterns of stars above her repeating? She doesn't have time to wonder how that's even possible.

Now that Sorrel is focusing on something outside the car, she's also noticing something she hasn't before: the neighbors. It's dark out now, and she can see the houses glowing from the inside. In every single available window, there's a face looking out at them. Sometimes two or three. She can't catch any details, only enough to see that they're all standing still, silhouettes in their windows, watching them scream through the neighborhood in John's stolen car.

"The hell is wrong with your neighbors?" Sorrel asks. Even though she's told herself no other questions matter, this one is beginning to seem like it does. She thinks about how John threatened her, about how Maud warned her, and fully realizes for the first time that because she's outside after the sun goes down, there are more dangers than just who or what John is.

This place is a sundown town. The neighbors must know. It's only a matter of time until they do something about it.

"They belong to him."

"The hell does that mean?"

One of the neighbors gives her an answer. As they drive by, an old white man with even whiter hair runs out onto his front lawn in nothing but tighty-whities. He grabs an ornamental gnome from his front garden and hurls it with all his might at the passing convertible. It strikes the hood, denting its surface.

"What the *fuck*?" Sorrel swerves. The wheels squeal. But she doesn't lose control.

Maud says, "He lets the men live here. So they're going to try to keep us here."

Sorrel has no time to parse whatever the fuck that means. Has, frankly, had enough of this whole goddamn neighborhood, so when one of John's neighbors shoots his pickup truck out into the street in an attempt to block them off, Sorrel just jumps the curb. She takes out the man's mailbox and a bed of flowers, has the car under control enough to flip the pickup driver the bird as she goes. The pickup just pivots and follows them, high beams glaring, engine roaring, American flag waving from a pole in its bed.

The neighborhood is riled up now. Sorrel can feel them all stirring, can see lights coming on in windows where they weren't before. People are coming out of their houses, taking to their lawns, shining bright lights and throwing things at the passing convertible, even if they have no hope of hitting it.

It's only a matter of time until one of them has a gun, Sorrel thinks. She knows. Wherever this place is, it's still America.

"Maud, tell me the way out of here."

But Maud says nothing. She's retreated into her seat, her eyes closed. Knees pulled up to her chest. Muttering to herself.

"Maud!" But Sorrel's raised voice only causes her to retreat further, to sink deeper down into her seat. "Maud, I'm sorry," she says, this time with her voice lowered. She eases off the accelerator as much as she can with the pickup gaining on them, takes her hand off the wheel and reaches over to grab Maud's knee. "Maud, baby, I need you to help me out here. I need you to tell me where to go. If we keep driving around in circles they're going to trap us. We'll hit a cul-de-sac or something. I need you to tell me where to go."

It's an agonizingly-long time before Maud finally squeaks out, in a nothing voice, "*The river.*"

"Which way is the river?"

"It's everywhere. It's all around the town. It's a moat. It's what keeps us trapped."

"A bridge, then."

A beat. Then. "That way!" Maud points to the right and Sorrel cranks the wheel, slamming on the accelerator, evolving their escape into a full-blown car chase. Multiple vehicles have piled up in pursuit, and Trinity Springs residents ahead have taken to their lawns, to the street, building improvised roadblocks with their own cars. Sorrel avoids them all, jumping up onto curbs, smashing through mailboxes and trash cans and flower beds, trenching yards and blasting through white picket-fences in their escape. Maud directs her from the passenger's seat, wind blowing through their hair as they drive.

"There's going to be a bridge," Maud says, her voice sounding like she's coming back to herself now. She yells over the sound of screeching tires and shooting wind and screaming neighbors. "If we can make it over the bridge we'll be okay. We'll be back home. But it's guarded."

"Guarded?"

"It's always guarded."

Sorrel doesn't have time to figure out by whom or what, pushes the convertible to its limit. She can smell the water before she sees the bridge.

It's an old, rusted truss bridge over a river that must be deep and strong, judging by the fact that she can hear it even with the wind and the tires and the engine. There are warning signs up over the bridge, as if it's undergoing construction. A lone man stands in front of the bridge, and just from his silhouette, Sorrel can tell he has a rifle. He holds it, stock on his hip, but doesn't fire.

Not yet.

They're so close. They're so goddamn close.

Sorrel eyes the road on the other side of the river. It looks like there's something wrong there. It's wriggling like a heat shimmer, a hallucination. It hurts Sorrel's eyes to look at, so she focuses back on the man guarding it.

"Maud, the bridge is one lane," she says, but not slowing down.

"I know."

The man fires the rifle into the air. Once.

Maud says, "It's the only way out."

The man levels the rifle.

"Get down!" Sorrel grabs Maud by the hair and shoves her down into her seat. She locks her left arm in place, keeping the convertible straight. Ducks down next to Maud.

The next shot blows out the windshield. Glass showers the inside of the convertible and Sorrel can feel the flying shards rip her arm apart, shred her dress, cut at her neck and the back of her head. Maud screams from her seat. But Sorrel keeps pushing forward.

There's a sickening bump and a distant *guh* and Sorrel knows she's struck the man and it's his body under the vehicle that spins the tires, jerks the wheel from her hand. There's an even more harrowing crash as metal slams into metal and they whip at a horrific angle and then the world is pulled out from underneath them as they're thrown out into the open air.

AMERICAN DREAM

It takes John awhile to readjust what remains of his face. There's a lot of pinching and pulling, a lot of prodding and preening for things to stay in place. It's not a painful process. Very little is painful for him anymore, thanks to this place. But it is an arduous one, and he now has a slightly better appreciation for why it takes Maud so long to put her makeup on every time they go out. When Maud kicked him, she tore the bottom half his face completely off; there's simply no fixing that. So when John is finally done readjusting, he appears to be good old John Kelly from the nose up.

Only the bottom half of his visage is amiss.

Where his mouth should be, where his chin isn't, there is a kind of hole. A black hole. A negative space in a way that doesn't make sense to look at. An emptiness that resists categorization, a blackness so black it sucks in even light.

John doesn't want to spend extra time looking for and reapplying the rest of his face, so he grabs an ascot from his closet and ties it around his face like a bandanna. It'll have to do for now.

When he finally makes it to the river, moving at a slow and steady walk, half of the husbands of Trinity Springs are there, looking down into the water. His convertible is ass-up on a sandbar, neither Maud nor Sorrel anywhere to be seen.

"Did they make it across?"

All the men jump at his presence.

"*Well?*"

A man nearby says, "We don't know, sir. All we know is they got Wedge." The man gestures and John's eyes follow. There's another husband splayed out in the grass by the bridge, clearly dead judging by the way his legs are all bent up and out of shape. Poor Wedge. He was a good man. Came here in '58 with his wife, Geraldine, tired of dealing with all the coloreds in his kids' schools. One of Trinity Springs's most senior residents.

John says, "Well, we'll pour one out for him," adjusting his cuffs.

They all stand there for another moment in awkward silence.

"I suggest you all get the hell out there and bring those cows back to me."

The sound of John Kelly's voice is enough to snap the residents of Trinity Springs into action.

Good thing he didn't have to show them his face.

THE STARS

It must be a dream.

It's too nice to be anything else. Sorrel's on her back, looking up at the stars. There's no feeling anymore. She remembers somewhere, distantly, pain, but it's a memory. A concept. It doesn't seem important now. Just like there used to be fear. She turns her head to the side, the rest of her body unable to obey her commands.

Maud.

Laid in the crook of her arm. Sleeping, just like they would before. In their old life. It takes a moment, but Sorrel finally manages to wrap her arm around Maud. Pulls her closer. Realizes they're under a blanket. Sorrel's...wet? It doesn't seem to matter when she tilts her head back up to look at the stars. The *moving* stars? The world all around them is moving.

No. What she's on is not a bed, but a boat.

Sorrel lifts her head, feeling the wet dress clinging to her body, droplets running down her face, and sees another shape with them. She panics, trying to move as she shape comes closer, but it doesn't mean her harm.

"You're alright. You're okay."

It's the woman from the waiting room.

Kate. With freckles of blood dotting her face.

"Don't worry. I won't let him get you."

And then Sorrel loses consciousness again.

part 4

Main Course

YOU ARE WHAT YOU EAT

Sorrel is still the next time she wakes. Not moving. No longer stars, but a ceiling above her. No hard wood under her back, but a soft mattress. It takes a truly horrendous amount of energy to move, to merely roll over, but she needs to. She feels body heat next to her, the shape of another person, and she needs to confirm.

It's Maud.

The first thing, the most important thing, is that Sorrel can hear Maud's breathing. It's ragged, sounds watery, but it's there. Her chest rises and falls. She's alive. Sorrel sees a few superficial wounds on Maud's face and remembers the car crash, remembers the river. It doesn't feel like anything's broken, but when Sorrel pulls back the blanket and looks down at her body, it sure looks like it is. She does the same on Maud's side of the bed, looking her over.

Their wounds have been attended to amateurishly but competently. Their dresses from Maud's house are still on, and Sorrel notices they've actually been laid on the bed above a layer of towels. Despite this, the whole bed is still covered in dirt and river grime, just like them. Bandages and gauze have been plastered onto their various wounds. She doesn't see any splints or anything; no major, gaping wounds. She's not a doctor, but guesses these are all good signs.

"Baby." Sorrel reaches over and touches Maud on the shoulder. It seems like the only place on her that isn't injured. "Baby, wake up. Maud, we've got to get out of here."

Maud stirs, pain on her face like she's running through a nightmare, and Sorrel tries again.

Just as there's a knock on the door.

Maud's eyes shoot open, full of horror. She looks up at Sorrel, whispers, *"Don't let him in."*

But it isn't John's voice they hear on the other side of the door. It cracks an inch, but doesn't open. Just enough to let the voice on the other side carry into the room. No peering eyes.

"Are you awake?" a woman asks. "Are you decent?"

Sorrel recognizes the voice. She doesn't know where from, though. She bounds out of bed, her whole body aching, sore. Even so, swiping the closest heavy object into her hands—a rotary telephone from the bedside table.

Whoever is on the other end of the door must think it's okay to let themselves in due to the commotion, and cracks the door just a bit more, poking her head through. Sorrel raises the telephone like a weapon, but when she sees who it is, wonders if she'll need to.

The woman from the waiting room. Kate.

It all comes back to her now. The car. The river. The boat.

"You." She says it with part shock, part relief, part accusation.

Kate's eyes widen as she looks at the rotary phone in Sorrel's grip, but she doesn't shy away. "May I come in?"

Sorrel looks at Maud, who's retreated to the headboard.

"You're not with him?" Sorrel asks.

Kate shakes her head. "No one knows you're here."

There's a moment of silence, and Kate seems to take it as an invitation to enter. She pushes the door open with a hip, and Sorrel sees she's carrying a tray with food on it. She sees apples, peaches, orange slices. Two glasses of iced tea. There's nothing that could even remotely be confused for meat. Sorrel doesn't know why that's so important to her all of a sudden, Maud told her not to eat *anything*.

Kate puts the tray down on the bed in front of Maud. It's able to stand up before her with the small legs on its underside. To Maud, she says, "Go ahead. It's not like what they give us. It's not from here."

Maud looks at Kate, and Sorrel can see a specific and hidden trust snap through their gazes. Not a language as secret as their own idioglossia, but the secret language all women share. Maud snatches food from the tray and starts wolfing it down. Sorrel doesn't know if she's ever seen anyone eat so greedily. Or, no, maybe that's not the right word. It implies a selfishness. Maud eats as if she hasn't eaten real food in years. Maybe she hasn't.

"My husband gets it for me sometimes," Kate says, "if he goes outside. As a present. If I'm…good…"

Sorrel clears her throat, drawing Kate's attention. "You saved us."

Kate seems embarrassed to admit to it. She looks down at the floor.

"How did you know?" Sorrel asks.

"I didn't." Kate shakes her head. "I was trying to get away too. I just happened to be there."

"So, you're not with him?" Sorrel asks again. After everything that's happened, she needs to be completely sure.

"It's not just him," Kate says. "It's all of them. *All* the men, the husbands. Well, most of them are husbands. But, to answer your question, no, I'm not with them. Us gals have to stick together, you know?"

Sorrel looks over at Maud on the bed, still eating. She seems to be coming back to herself now. Slowing down. Regaining color. Looking more and more like the Maud of yesteryear.

"Funny," Sorrel says. "You couldn't come to that conclusion before you sold me down the fucking river?"

Kate flinches as if Sorrel raised a hand, and when Sorrel sees that movement, all the anger instantly leaves her body. In that one small twitch Sorrel realizes how truly twisted this place is, the kind of person it turns someone into if they stay. "Kate, I'm—"

But Kate raises a hand to stop her, suddenly assertive. "No," she says, her face stern now. "Don't you dare apologize for being rightfully angry with me. Women have to apologize for simply existing. I knew what I was doing when I let you in. I knew what I was doing with this place."

Sorrel lets a long breath out. "That's fair. So...what is it, this place?"

Kate lets that question hang in the air for a frighteningly long time. Sorrel can see it on her face, plain as day; she's afraid. She's terrified not just of the answer, but of saying the answer out loud. Of telling someone else. Of confronting it, making it real.

"It's his place," Kate says. "It's like he's God here. I don't know how to explain what it is. It's here, but not here. It's not on any map. It moves. All across the country. Maybe the world, I'm not sure. He can go out and end up anywhere he pleases. Sometimes he lets the men go out. Bachelors looking for wives. It's almost impossible to find Trinity Springs from the outside unless you're invited."

Sorrel didn't want to think about how that made sense. But somehow it did.

"He's in charge of everything here. He makes it looks like he wants it to."

Sorrel scoffs. Give a straight white man the power to make his own utopia and of course he'd move it back in time. America for ya.

"And what about Kelly?" she asks. "What is he? I hit him. I hit him with a meat tenderizer, but he didn't stay down. I hit him and he... There's...something *beneath* him." She really does struggle to put into words what exactly she saw beneath John's skin. She remembers Maud hitting him, remembers that wet slapping sound as the piece of his scalp hit the bathroom wall. She wonders if it's still there now, slowly dripping down the tile. But she also remembers striking him herself, remembers bringing the tenderizer down on his head hard enough to crack skull. A blow that should've killed a man. Remembers pulling Maud away from him, him still grabbing at her despite his wounds, despite that canyon in his face.

And the nothingness beyond it.

Kate says, "There's something within all of us. But...not him."

"But he is a man?" Sorrel says, realizing it comes out not as a statement but a question.

"He is a man," Kate says. "All men are the same, I guess."

"But how..."

Kate shrugs. "I don't know. Sometimes there's just nothing inside someone. No heart."

"So that story about him finding this place," Sorrel says, "is it true?"

For the first time, through a mouthful of food, Maud speaks up. "It's the same story he told me when we met." The sound of her voice seems to wash the blood and fear away from Sorrel. She literally feels a layer of something peel off of her as she looks to the bed, sees Maud sitting there. Her clothes are ripped to shreds and she's covered in wounds and gore and river grime and running makeup and apple juice, but good fucking god she's the most beautiful thing Sorrel has ever seen.

Maud smiles when she looks back at Sorrel, and it's a real smile. One that reaches her eyes. Her beautiful green eyes.

"Hey, dollface."

Sorrel throws herself across the bed and into Maud's arms. Forgetting completely about Kate. About the tray of food she bashes her knee on and knocks over. Nothing else matters except Maud. Sorrel hugs her hard with the intent to crush her, to pull her into her own body and make them one, so that they're never separated again.

"Can't breathe!"

"Don't care." Sorrel loosens her grip just enough to allow breath, but she doesn't let go. Only gives Maud enough breathing room so that she can look down into her eyes.

"What happened to you? How did you get here?"

Maud gathers herself.

"John was telling the truth with his little meet-cute story. Kind of."

"*Church?*" Sorrel can't imagine it.

Maud scoffs. "The *basement* of a church."

AA? NA? What had happened to her since they've been apart? Sorrel imagines some version of what happened to her. Drifting. Aimless. Doing anything to feel a feeling.

"He said he came to be part of the group," Maud said. "He didn't dress like he does now, but even then I knew it was a lie. Even walking in there in jeans and a button-down, I knew he was too rich. I could smell it on him. All that was just a lie anyway. He just came to scope people out. And not just women. Like she said, the men who live here, they're people too. They *choose* to be here. He gives them obedient wives and they give him their obedience. They get to live in *paradise*." She practically spits the word out.

Sorrel leans back slightly, horrified. Out of the corner of her eye she looks at Kate, who simply nods, confirming. "You?"

Kate nods again. "My husband Gary brought me here. Our first house after we got married."

Sorrel didn't want to ask the next question, but did it anyway. "When was that?"

"1967. I loved the neighborhood. It reminded me of my childhood." Kate clearly sees the look of horror on Sorrel's face, because the next thing she does is slightly raise a hand and say, "Don't tell me. Please, just... I don't want to know. Just in case we don't make it out of here. I'd rather not know."

"I don't understand," Sorrel says, leaning against the bed. "All these women. The people we saw cutting the grass and taking care of the lawns. The—the fucking cook in your house! They're all trapped here? How does he do it?" She realizes she's asked the question, but just as soon realizes she has the answer. How have people been trapped in situations like that before? It's happened over and over again throughout time. It would be easy to replicate. Especially if you had some strange not-neighborhood where escape seemed next to impossible. That seems as good an answer as any.

But Kate gives a different one.

"It's the food," she says.

Sorrel thinks of the feast John laid out for them, how insistent he seemed to be to get her to eat, to drink her drink.

She thinks about the pomegranate seeds.

"You did that to get me here," she says, looking at Maud, who merely nods. Sorrel hesitates. "So, if it's the food, then what's that meat? That's not anything I've ever seen before."

This time, Maud answers.

"It's us."

Sorrel looks at her, thinking about the disgusting meat smell. Her mouth goes moist, but because there's bile creeping up the back of her throat. She thinks of the thing in the tub. Of *her*.

"You...*what*?" She doesn't want to know, so why is she pushing?

There's a dark look in Maud's eyes. "The bathroom."

She remembers it climbing out of the tub, legs wobbling like a newborn deer.

"They're us. Our insides. Everything we have to give up in order to stay here."

Sorrel's going to vomit again. She prays if she does, it's actual vomit this time.

Maud breathes deep, tells her, "They're everything we repress. Everything we wanna be, but everything we can't, because we're here. This place, it...it doesn't allow it. Everything that makes us different, we have to push back down." She looks deeply into Sorrel's eyes. "You know what happens when you try to repress something."

It always comes up again.

"Jesus fuck," Sorrel gasps, unable to string together anything more articulate.

Maud says, "And when they come up, they have to go down again."

Sorrel starts, but doesn't finish. Her brain catches up with her mouth and she dry heaves, doubling over at the thought. There's nothing in her stomach but acid. It doesn't come up entirely, merely burning the back of her throat. That was why Maud told her not to eat anything. That was why the meat smelled so bad. Like roadkill.

"Sometimes after a while you can feel it coming back. The old you. The *you* you were like on the outside. That's when your husband makes you eat."

Sorrel breathes, tries to get herself under control. She looks at Kate. "What does that mean about you? You haven't..." She can't actually say it out loud.

Kate shakes her head. "Not in a while. Long enough for me to remember what this place really is."

"And your husband didn't know?"

"Women don't need to be a good liars to lie to a man. They hear what they want to hear."

Sorrel knows that much is true, but she still looks over at Maud, tries to gauge her thoughts on the situation. She gives Sorrel a single, slow nod.

"Plus," Kate adds, "my husband is dead. I killed him. Or, anyway, the other me."

"Another... Where is she?" Maud asks.

Kate gestures over her shoulder as if it were the simplest answer in the world. "In the other room." She pushes the door open quietly, and they can see, lying on the couch, sleeping under a thick blanket, another Kate. It's difficult to tell it's the same woman, devoid of all her makeup as she is, but Sorrel recognizes that hair, the shape of the face.

Kate pulls the door closed.

"So, she's leaving with us?" Maud asks, as if it were the most normal thing in the world to simply skate past the presence of someone's doppelgänger. For her, it was.

"I fuckin' guess," Sorrel says, because this is just the territory they're in now. "So, how do we?" she asks, looking between Kate and Maud. "Make it out of here, I mean. The river? Is that the only way?"

Maud nods. "The bridge is the only safe way. And there's only one. The river..." She looks across the room to Kate.

"What?" Sorrel asks, hating the thought of their escape being bottlenecked. "What's wrong with the river?"

"There's a current," Maud says.

"So we swim it. We can do it."

"No, not like that." Maud shakes her head. "So, you know a normal current, how you jump into a river and by the time you climb up onto the other bank you're a bit downriver? It's like that. Only you don't know where you'll come out. Or—"

Please don't say what I think you're gonna say, Sorrel thinks.

"—when."

Fuck.

"He showed us once," Kate says. "With one of his gardeners who got caught stealing. We watched him..." She lifts her hand to her mouth, unable to continue.

"You don't need to tell me," Sorrel says. She can figure it out on her own, tries not to imagine the sight of someone vanishing into that haze on the other side of the river. Tries to simply label what happened as *death* without imagining the implications, what exactly happened to the body when it was thrown through some horrible cosmic tunnel. "What about your rowboat?"

"My husband's fishing boat," Kate says. "I didn't know if that was going to work. I was going to try to stay under the bridge and hope for the best."

"So the bridge is the only bet," Sorrel says, looking at them both for confirmation. They nod. Easy enough on its face. "But it's definitely blockaded by now. All the other people who live in this neighborhood. They're like you two? They're trapped here too?"

"Some," Maud says. "Not all. The men are the ones who want to stay here. But the wives and the servants, yeah."

"Well, we can't just leave them here."

"I'm assuming you have a plan, then?"

"I'm beginning to."

KEEP TRINITY SPRINGS GREAT

John puts the finishing touches on replacing his face, looking at himself in the mirror, making sure it's all on straight, that nothing is amiss. Yes, he still looks like the handsome, debonair man he intended this skin to be. A couple tucks around the neck, the skin equivalent of straightening his tie, and everything is where it should be.

John goes into the kitchen and finds a cocktail waiting for him, another old fashioned. It's better than Maud's, better than the ones he makes for himself. Of course it is. This is their whole job. And he didn't even see them making it, didn't even hear them as they stealthily left the room before he entered. Seen and not heard, and sometimes not even seen. Perfection.

John sips slowly, trying to calm himself, looking out into the back garden as he does. In the dark of night, he can see his expansive backyard, his territory. The yard is his, but it all belongs to him, really, the entire neighborhood. The husbands will find the girls eventually. There's no place they can go where someone won't find them. If worse came to worse, John could even enlist the help of the help. Offer a reward. He knows from experience those people will turn against their own kind if given the proper incentive. It happened before. And when he got them back, he'd put the girls in their places. Maud back at his side, and Sorrel where she belonged.

John already decided she would stay in the house, unlike the rest of the help, who have their own apartments on the edge of town. He has her room all figured out. The guest room on the first floor, the other end of the house. It's perfect, has access to its own private bathroom, is closer to the kitchen, the stairs, giving Sorrel access to the laundry room. And on the other end of the house means it would be some distance from Maud when he decides to go help himself to her one night.

John Kelly would be far from the only man in Trinity Springs who acted in a way that was counter to how he behaved. Despite everything he's said about those he refers to as *the lesser races*, John has found himself attracted to them from time to time. He thinks even Thomas Jefferson had some mulatto children.

John walks into the dining room, taking his drink with him. He picks his fork off his plate and spears a particularly juicy piece of meat right off the serving plate, wolfs it down. It goes down easy, lovely, and he has another. And another. And another. Careful not to drip any on his nice suit.

After a few bites of his wife, John is satisfied, feels a delicious warmth in his stomach. Throughout history, savages got a lot wrong, but there was one thing they got very right; eating was a powerful act. You could absorb the strength of another person through eating, and eating those little pieces of Maud, John feels her resistance, her determination. It buoys his own, and he moves into the sitting room, turns on the radio, sits, and listens.

Each of the cars in Trinity Springs has a radio, and some of those cars have walkie-talkies in them. That way the residents can all report anything strange, anything out of the ordinary. His own little neighborhood watch, where everyone is their own policeman. A perfect panopticon.

But what John hears on the radio now is incoherent. It doesn't make sense. The husbands are all supposed to be out there looking for his wife and her little friend. But they're seemingly everywhere. By the bridge at the wreckage of his car. At the park. Running down the middle of a street in the direction of John's house. It doesn't make sense. Nobody's that fast.

Not unless they could suddenly be in multiple places at once.

He shoots up and out of his chair.

REVOLUTION

Trinity Springs has descended into complete chaos. People run the streets cheering and howling, but they're largely the *same* people. The same three women. Copies of them are spotted all over town. A blond, a redhead, and a light-skinned, curly-haired brunette. The endless repetitions of the three women are all naked and covered in some sort of sludge, running and howling like banshees as the neighborhood cowers in terror of them.

Ripping up flowerbeds, knocking over flagpoles.

Working together to overturn cars.

Uprooting mailboxes.

Pelting rocks through windows.

Some of them take shits right on front stoops. They smear mud across white picket fences and kick the boards in. A couple push two fingers up inside themselves, and then scrawl obscenities on the bay windows of houses in their own blood. One blond and one brunette are furiously fucking in the middle of the street, bedded down on top of an American flag.

And as they are all doing this, they are all free.

Just as the neighborhood watch begins rallying to get a handle on the chaos, just as they're beginning to realize something strange is afoot, that all these women are the same and they're not an army of foreign invaders who've somehow crossed the river, yet more women join the copies of the three. Copies that are not Sorrel or Maud or Kate but the various wives of Trinity Springs. They come bursting out of back doors and cellars and attic windows, a fury unleashed on the town that's unlike anything it's ever seen. These copies, too, are not just doubles, but triples, quadruples, infinitesimals. All brought forth, all crawling their way to the surface, to reality, upon seeing the miniature uprising.

The original Sorrel and Maud move through the backyards of Trinity Springs amidst all that chaos.

They've changed out of their soiled and soaking dinner dresses and into clothes pilfered from Kate's husband's closet. Sorrel feels much more like herself in baggy cargo pants, an oversized tank top, and boots. Maud doesn't exactly feel at home in Kate's tracksuit and sneakers, but it's certainly better than the doll outfits John forced her to wear.

"It's working," Sorrel says, though not knowing why she's whispering. There's more than enough noise, enough chaos, to cover their movements. "It's working!" Women are running, screaming, all over town. Engines roar and radios squawk. External floodlights on houses come on, streetlights and headlights lighting up the night. People are running everywhere, screaming and shouting, the copies of the Trinity Springs women running, pursued by the men. Some of the men have seemingly given up trying to catch their own wives and just put their hands on any woman they find, keeping them prisoner. No lasting harm comes to any of them. At least not yet; no one is sure of who is a double and who is real.

They took a chance thinking this would work, making their own doubles and hoping they would stir something inside the hearts of Trinity Springs's wives. It was a chance Sorrel knew would pay off; she thought about every time something stirred within herself when she was younger and she saw something out of the heteronorm. She knew what it was like to have something buried, knew no matter how deep you think you hid it, it was really only ever under a couple inches of soil. Whether that thing was a love for your best friend or a dissatisfaction with a supposedly-perfect life, it never stayed buried.

And yet in all that morass, all that confusion, Sorrel sees one sight that punches a hole through that glee. A small woman, dressed like a Trinity Springs housewife, complete with an apron, stands in the back of a pickup truck, looking over the various women who are brought before her. She's shaking with fury and tottering atop her high heels, looking like she's about to fall over, as she glares down into their faces.

"What the fuck?" Sorrel gasps, but Maud pulls at her, doesn't let her stay long. It's difficult for Sorrel to look away from this, but it seems so easy for Maud. Sorrel doesn't want to think about the horrors Maud witnessed in here that would've made her numb to something like this. "The hell was that?" she asks, not really expecting an answer. Really, knowing the answer.

There will always be people who prefer cages to freedom.

BE A MAN ABOUT IT

Sorrel and Maud crouch in the bushes, looking into John's backyard. She has a plan, and she's beginning to realize how insane and far-fetched it is. But it's the only plan they have. Their only shot. They could just leave, sure. Try to get past the bridge. Maybe try Kate's plan of using the boat and see where that got them. But even if they got away, John, all the other husbands, Trinity Springs itself, it would still be out there. All the people they'd kidnapped would still be out there. And they knew they wouldn't be able to live long with that.

"Are you ready?" Sorrel asks.

Maud doesn't say anything, just reaches out and grabs Sorrel by the back of the head, gets herself a handful of hair. She pulls her in close, mashes their faces together for a hard, powerful kiss. There's love in it, yes, and also years of pent-up desire, and also the thought that if this is it, if it is the end, that at least they're going to go out doing something right.

Just like they had been all along.

They creep through the backyard and open the sliding glass door at the back of the house. They can hear the radio on in another room, the sounds of men from all around Trinity Springs calling in sightings of doppelgänger women, some they know, some they don't. They creep slowly, splitting up to come around into the living room from different angles. Sorrel is momentarily despondent as she loses sight of Maud, but then she's there again, on the other side of the living room.

And John is on the couch between them.

Sorrel approaches slowly, quietly, the knife she brought from Kate's kitchen raised. She quickly grabs John by the back of the head, yanks it back. Exposing his neck. She raises the knife. And looks down at a John Kelly, one whose eyes are lifeless as a doll's.

"He's a double."

That's when the kitchen lights come on.

"After everything I've done?" John steps into the living room, silhouetted by the backlight as he peels his suit jacket off. His face is repaired, the vacuous hole covered. He rolls up his sleeves. He looks at Maud. "After everything I've given you?" He looks at Sorrel. "Everything you could've had?" He doesn't wait for their response, as usual. "Just goes to show you we really should just close down our borders."

"Not gonna call for reinforcements?" Sorrel asks.

"No," John says, tucking his tie in between the buttons of his shirt. "This stays in the family."

At least they could count on him to be a man about it.

Maybe, because of that, they had a chance.

NOTHING UNDERNEATH

John's hand shoots out and grabs Sorrel by the throat. His grip is powerful. Tyrannical. The most intense thing Sorrel has ever felt. And then she's in his face. That sneering, awful face. Looking into his eyes, Sorrel sees that same nothingness that was the black hole beneath his features. A complete absence of anything.

"You sneak in in the middle of the night like a rodent," he growls into her face, his breath like spoiled meat. God, it's that same sick roadkill smell from dinner. He's been eating it. Eating *Maud*. "You cross my borders, you seduce and defile my wife. And then you try to *kill me*?"

Then Maud is on him. She screams and throws herself onto his back, but it's like tackling a building. John barely moves. Even as she stabs him in the back with Kate's kitchen knife. His arm twists around in an impossible position, moving like it's jointless, like there really is nothing inside him, a snake coiling back over itself, and snatches Maud by the throat as well. He pulls Maud over his shoulder so that he's gripping both the women in front of him, arms extended, holding them above the ground like they weigh nothing.

"And you. You ungrateful cow."

He tosses Sorrel aside. She hits the couch, flips over it, her knee cracking the double John Kelly in the shoulder. She rolls at an awkward angle into the floor. At least she can breathe again.

"I gave you everything," John says, holding Maud with both hands now. "I took care of you. I fed you. I made sure you wanted for *nothing*. What else could you have wanted?" John lifts her higher like he's going to throw her.

Sorrel looks at the other John, the double on the couch who hasn't moved during the fight. Its eyes are still clouded over. There's an absence there. She doesn't know if it's simply like that, or if that's what happens to these doubles after a while. She remembers what Kate said, that there's just nothing in some people. Maybe this one had never been anything at all.

Sorrel pulls herself to her feet, picking up the closest thing to throw. It's the radio, which smashes uselessly against the side of John's head. All the strike manages to do is tear away another flap of skin, and Sorrel can see that horrible, black emptiness in there again.

John says, "Don't worry," but his mouth doesn't move. Not his human mouth anyway. Whatever speaks, it comes from inside that blackness, its voice deep and foundational, shaking Sorrel's bones. "You'll get your turn, mulatto," John growls, lowering Maud just a little so he can drop his shoulder and slide sideways, slam into

Sorrel. He knocks her back but not down, and she grabs a TV tray and throws it into his legs.

That finally knocks him off balance. He goes down, letting go of Maud as he reaches out to stop his fall.

Maud gulps for air, but Sorrel cannot let up the attack. She grabs her dropped knife and stabs down into his bicep, cutting all the way through him and into the hardwood floor. But there's something wrong. It doesn't have the resistance she thinks muscle and bone should. Instead, it feels like she cut through papier mâché, through cardboard. Like there really is nothing beneath him.

"Darkie bitch!" John screams, rolling away, tearing his entire arm off as he goes. It comes free like a sleeve, not a limb, and just as hollow. Sorrel looks at the stump, at where there should be blood and broken bone shining through, but she only sees that pitch. That hole. Like staring out into a starless night. When he looks at Sorrel, his face is wrong, tilted, and the darkness is there too.

"It's fine," he says, composing himself. "It's fine. I can always get another one."

He hauls back and kicks Sorrel in the face, his form like a football punter, her head at just the wrong angle. She feels her neck snap backwards, feel a twinge in there somewhere, something torquing—please God not breaking—that she knows shouldn't, and she flops down onto her back, staring up at the ceiling, everything ringing, everything doubled.

Sorrel is distantly aware of Maud somewhere out there, of John, of him coming over to grab her, haul her to her feet. But there's nothing she can do about it. She wills her limbs to move, but she can only lie there, prostrate, and watch as John bends down to grab Maud, as he rolls her over onto her stomach and plants a foot in the center of her back.

"Why don't you tell her?" he says, his voice distant, like it's coming from the bottom of a well. "Why don't you tell her, sweetheart, how this was all your idea? How you wanted to invite her for dinner?"

Sorrel can feel blood running down her face. She looks across the room at Maud, lying on the ground, covered in blood and scrapes and bruises. She thinks about what she thought was the last time she'd ever thought she'd see her; framed by her bedroom window years ago. The side of the house had always been an easy way for them to come and go as they pleased. Maud looked much the same then. God, Sorrel hopes this isn't the last time she sees her now.

"Tell her!" John screams.

Beneath him, Maud takes a deep breath.

"I... I wanted you here." She winces as John steps harder into her back. "I didn't care how. I didn't care what it meant for you, even if it meant..." She looks around the room and Sorrel knows exactly what she means. She didn't care if this place was inflicted upon her. "I just wanted to see you. I just wanted the chance for us to be together. Even if it was a small chance. Even if it was a nothing chance."

What's left of John's face smiles and he looks over at Sorrel.

"You see? You're not here to save her." He stoops down and grabs Maud with his one remaining arm. "You're here to *serve us.*" He hauls Maud off the floor like she weighs nothing. Like she's a child. "It is *us,*" he says, looking at her. "Isn't it?" Maud is a doll in his hands, struggling but ineffective.

"Fuck you!" Maud pulls back and kicks him square in the crotch. But it has no effect. Figures.

John sighs. "That's fine. I can always get another one of you. Even when I got you, you were a low-value woman."

The clacking of heels on kitchen tile suddenly interrupts them, and all three of them turn to see the maid standing in the kitchen doorway. She stands in her usual position, hands clasped before her, looking down at the floor.

"Just in time," John says, "there's going to be a mess for you to attend to."

The maid lifts her head, and even from where she lies on the ground, Sorrel can see a spark in her eyes that wasn't there before.

"You have guests," she says, and then adds "*sir,*" with more venom than Sorrel has ever heard poured into a word.

"Of course, I kn..." John suddenly turns towards the front door. Sorrel follows his gaze and sees another Maud standing in the doorway to the foyer, stark naked, covered in bloody slime, and armed with nothing but her own two hands.

"No," John says. He looks back at the Maud he's holding. "*You're* her."

But then another Maud steps in through the front door. Followed by two Sorrels. And then more dark-skinned faces John doesn't recognize. He can't recognize them, after all. He's never bothered to learn them, despite the fact that he's taken them, that he sees them every day, that they keep everything he has running. And in a flash, they're everywhere. Copies of Maud and Sorrel and Kate, other women from Trinity Springs, the servants from various houses and yards and streets, everyone devoid of the attire that separates them, all naked as the day they were born.

Tonight. Moments ago.

The plan was working.

John drops the real Maud, spinning in circles, realizing he's surrounded. There's no fear on what's left of that face, but there is realization.

"What are you doing here?" he asks them all, his voice altered like he's trying to speak with something in his mouth.

None of them answer.

"How dare you enter my house?"

Each one of them steps closer.

"No!" John spins and spins, but there's nowhere to go, realizing escape in every direction is cut off. "You can't do this! This is *my* house!"

The original Maud crawls across the floor, comes closer to Sorrel, lifts her head up.

"Can you move?"

Sorrel doesn't think anything is broken, but she still shakes her head.

"It's alright," Maud says, ducking under her arm. "I've got you." But she very clearly doesn't, can't get her up off the floor.

A dark hand reaches down.

The maid.

Sorrel takes her hand and the maid helps pull her to her feet.

"Head on out," she says, kindness in her eyes. "We can take care of him."

As Maud helps carry Sorrel away, the army of doubles, triples, quadruples, piles into the house, surges towards John. More and more of them coming in at every moment, practically trampling over one another to get him, a ravenous horde. John shouts, a monstrous, hissing roar that turns quickly to screams as the army descends upon him.

part 5
Digestif

BURN IT DOWN AND SALT THE GROUND

Maud drags Sorrel out into the backyard, where there are even more women, even more brown faces. They've surrounded the house, coming from yards all around Trinity Springs to look upon the place that's plagued them all, the place that will soon become little more than a memory. The sounds of violence throughout the neighborhood have slowed, nearly stopped. John's screams, too, have died out.

HOME

Sorrel leans her head back against the headrest and watches the exact same house whip by again and again. Many of them are deserted. Some of them are on fire. Naked people watch from the streets. Trinity Springs is emptying. She can hear motors all around them as they drive through the cookie-cutter streets towards the bridge.

Sorrel passes out for a moment, and when she's awake she can smell the river.

"We're almost there," Maud says, "almost home."

She's out again, and when she opens her eyes they've stopped. She tilts her head, can see the metal of the truss bridge to her right, in the distance. There's a group of people heading towards it. The world around Sorrel seems to wobble, lose focus.

"This is it," Maud says. "We're going home."

Sorrel summons all of her strength and grabs Maud by the front of her shirt, pulls her in close, and kisses her bruised and bloody lips, her heart doing backflips the entire time.

GLIMPSE

When the sun rises over the town of Beacon, it's different than most days. Most of the town's residents don't even see it. After all, to glimpse what happens, you have to be at a very specific angle; near the shore of the lake, looking out over the water. The few that are manage to convince themselves of a rare-but-somehow-explainable occurrence. It must be something about the way the reflection of the sun hits the water, something that makes it look like fire, like an explosion. Like when sailors of old would see those green flashes of light. After all, there's no noise to accompany the light show. Just like a sunrise, albeit redder than usual, hotter, faster, more intense. So the few who are there watch it, and they enjoy it, and then, when the light show is over, they jump into action, seeing that there are somehow *people* out there on the lake.

Bobbing to the surface. Swimming for the shore.

Acknowledgments

It's weird to write an acknowledgements page to a book for a second time, but also lucky, in a way. Some people may know this novella was originally published by Off Limits Press in October of 2024. Waylon sent me my first ever novella acceptance and worked so hard to make it such a special occasion, so I don't consider this a revised or expanded or director's cut-y version or material that was missing from the original version.

If you happened to pick up that edition while it was in print, you'll see some changes, sure, but I view them as my personal changes as a writer and a person, not about any perceived imperfections of the original book.

So in addition to Waylon, and to btrcp who did the astounding cover art for the original version, there are all the people to thank for both the original edition of *The Familialists*, as well as everyone involved with this return to life.

Obviously, there's David-Jack and the Slashic fam to thank for picking it up for a second round, and for taking such good care of a book that had already seen the light of day once. Big emotional support thanks to the GTTUnit and my own personal Horror

Writer Group, as always, for being a constant source of fun and spookiness, and to Mike Barron for helping with the earliest feedback on this book, and helping me tone it down, which made it all the more terrifying.

About the author

TT Madden (they/them) is a Pushcart-nominated, genderfluid, mixed-race writer who refuses to keep "politics" out of their writing. They've written in the sandboxes of big IPs, helping create a *Blair Witch* tabletop mystery game, but they much prefer writing smaller, weirder stories that make you uncomfortable, but in a way you hopefully want to explore more.

Their short prose has been published by Ghoulish Tales, Bag of Bones Press, and Speculation Publications, among others. Their novellas have been published by Off Limits Press, Neon Hemlock, Mad Axe Media, and Little Ghost Books, with more forthcoming.

They can be found at ttmaddenwrites.carrd.co when they're not wandering the woods around their home, looking for spooky inspiration.